PUFFIN BOOKS

STARLIGHT ADVENTURE 3:
ISLAND OF SECRETS

Determined to escape from your humdrum life back home, your boring boyfriend and your nagging mother, you take the plunge and set off for the sun-drenched island of Simnos, in Greece, to work through the summer as a villa girl. After a few days, something makes you realize that beautiful, bustling Simnos has a secret – one which has lain hidden for hundreds of years – the location of the legendary and fabulous treasure of Aphrodite, goddess of love. But as you begin your careful search, it soon becomes clear that someone else is searching for the gold too – someone who is prepared to be utterly unscrupulous!

Could it be the gorgeous windsurfer, Panos Pavlides? Could it be the mysterious Englishman, Garth Craigmillar? Or could it be someone infinitely more dangerous?

As you are swept up into this thrilling treasure hunt, all you have to do is to make the choices, decide which course to travel and who to trust. And if you are lucky – or very clever – you just might solve the mystery of the *Island of Secrets*!

Kim Jordan

STARLIGHT ADVENTURE 3:

Island of Secrets

Illustrated by Peter Wilks

Puffin Books

Thanks to Sue Muddiman,
Ian Jenkins and Jeanne Hales

Puffin Books, Penguin Books Ltd, Harmondsworth, Middlesex, England
Viking Penguin Inc., 40 West 23rd Street, New York, New York 10010, U.S.A.
Penguin Books Australia Ltd, Ringwood, Victoria, Australia
Penguin Books Canada Ltd, 2801 John Street, Markham, Ontario, Canada L3R 1B4
Penguin Books (N.Z.) Ltd, 182–190 Wairau Road, Auckland 10, New Zealand

First published 1985

Made and printed in Great Britain by
Cox & Wyman Ltd, Reading
Filmset in 11/13pt Linotron Palatino by
Rowland Phototypesetting Ltd
Bury St Edmunds, Suffolk

INTRODUCTION

You, the heroine of this adventure, are looking for your first full-time job. You're not at all sure what kind of work you want to do. Your most positive desire is to escape from the shabby south-coast resort where you live with your domineering mother and your elder sister. Your mother is keen for you to settle down and is pressurizing you to take a clerical job in a local insurance company, which a friend of the family has set up for you. Your unwillingness to give in to her is strengthened by the fact that your long-standing boyfriend, Nigel, also works for the accounts department of the same firm.

Then, one afternoon, you spot an advert in the *Daily Mail*:

VILLALINK LTD
Villa girls needed immediately
mid June to end September
Apply Box 207

and on an impulse you apply.

Your application is successful and a week later your mother reluctantly agrees to your joining ten other girls your age on the Villalink training course. At the end of the course you are delighted to be told that you have passed and that your first assignment will be in a large villa on the Greek island of Simnos, in the Aegean, not all that far from Crete.

You travel home in a happy haze, only to be greeted by a renewed barrage of protests from your mother, who insists that you are too young to embark on such an unpredictable venture. With considerable tact, you talk her into reluctant acceptance and by the end of the week you are on the way to Greece, your first real job, and adventure!

HOW TO PLAY

Your adventure begins at the first reference, when you arrive in glorious, sunny Greece. From there on, you make all the choices, all the decisions. But beware! Not all your choices will be the right ones.

Luck and Fate

Greece is, according to the legends, the land of the gods – a land where choice may be taken from you, while the Fates determine your next move. If the Fates are with you, you will be lucky. If they are not, bad luck will come your way. All you have to do is to roll a die, or choose any number between 1 and 6, and turn to the reference indicated. Sometimes you will be required to toss a coin.

You begin your adventure with ten Luck points. The number of points you acquire or lose during your adventure is important, so you should keep a record of your score somewhere. At the end of the adventure, you will be able to see how well you have done, and if you are unlucky the first time, you can try again, making different choices – and perhaps the Fates will be kinder!

YOUR ARRIVAL AT SIMNOS

The ferry boat shunts backwards and forwards, trying to dock in Simnos, a procedure which seems to take ages. Once the boat is firmly moored you shuffle down the gangplank with your fellow travellers and jostle your way towards a girl clutching a Villalink sign. She introduces herself as Penny, the other Villalink representative, who will be your companion for the next few months. She briskly summons a taxi – a battered old grey Mercedes – and you are soon rattling through the twistling lanes of the town. Spiros, the taxi driver, careers around sudden bends shouting greetings to all and sundry, while Penny talks at breakneck speed about her experiences as a villa girl in Corfu and Rhodes. Finally, Penny's chatter fades as you round a bend to find yourselves overlooking a lovely secluded inlet. A whitewashed villa with white balconies and blue shutters sits wedged against one side of the steep hill behind, facing seawards. You have your first glimpse of your home for the summer, the Villa To Limani . . .

Penny shows you to your room. It is small and spartan, but the spectacular view makes up for it. From the open window you can see right along the bay from Simnos town to the windmill at the top of the cliff path. The room also has the convenience of two entrances, one from the corridor, and the other from a flight of stone steps leading up the side of the villa. A few scattered belongings have been left by your predecessor – a dried-up stick of mascara, a tube of sticky suntan cream, a couple of unused postcards and a few paperbacks. You save the postcards and the books and throw the rest in the bin. Pulling out the top drawer of a wooden chest of drawers you discover a small pamphlet, crudely printed on plain white paper, its edges now yellow and curled up with time. On the front cover is a pen-and-ink illustration of what looks like a monastery with imposing domed towers, standing high on a mountain top surrounded by olive groves. Underneath the picture is written *The History of Simnos*. You put the pamphlet to one side while you finish unpacking, intending to come back to it later.

Your first task is to settle in the new guests. There are some short-stay guests and some long-stay, like the Chadwicks, who have arrived with two children, Mrs Chadwick's brother, Greg Lewis, and the grandmother, Irene Chadwick.

When everyone is safely installed you decide to do a quick tour of inspection to make sure they are all happy. Raised voices from Room 6 indicate that trouble is brewing. The door is open, so you peep cautiously into the room and ask if you can be of any assistance. Donna Chadwick, a well-groomed woman in her early thirties, with bright honey-blond hair and rather too much make-up, is standing, hands on hips, in the centre of the room.

'You most certainly *can* be of assistance, young lady. We've booked for a long holiday and when I book a room with an *en suite* bathroom, I expect to get what I pay for. Not a cubby-hole with a shower in it.'

Her husband Steve is fiddling with the suitcases, looking as though he wished the floor would swallow him up.

'Don't you dare unpack those bags, Steve,' orders Donna. 'We're not staying in this room. Unless you can offer us alternative accommodation we're going off to the most expensive hotel we can find, and Villalink can foot the bill . . .'

How will you handle this tricky situation?

Lay down the law and tell Donna she is being unreasonable	Turn to 25
Apologize profusely	Turn to 51

2

A look of disappointment briefly flits across his face and then it's gone. Penny looks astonished but you notice that Liam has perked up a little. You suddenly feel sick of the lot of them. Penny makes a move to go to the Black Cat but you decide to have an early night instead. Besides, you have to write home to your mother and, something you find you're not looking forward to, a letter should go to Nigel. You go back to the villa.

Turn to 324

3

'Clues as to the whereabouts of the missing tablets, of course,' says Liam. Seeing your blank looks, he beams, relishing the prospect of talking at some length about his great passion, archaeology.

'You must have heard of the scandal. Last year some tablets of marble taken from the Sanctuary of Aphrodite, and thought to depict in detail the structure of the temple, were stolen from Aghios Dionysus. The monks had kept them for centuries without realizing their value in archaeological terms. It was only when the project to excavate the ruins on Simnaki was announced that they mysteriously went missing from the monastery vaults. If only I could have had a glimpse at them, I'm sure my theory would be proven.'

'What theory is that, Liam?' asks Panos, stifling a yawn.

'The theory that the Sanctuary of Aphrodite at

Simnos houses some of the greatest treasures of ancient Greece. That's all. I've spent my last year at university working on a thesis to this effect. Unfortunately our excavations don't seem to be bearing out my hypothesis.'

'You mean you haven't found anything. To put it frankly,' you suggest, without too much tact.

'It's as if we've been jinxed. Our findings have been most routine. Thanks to our eminent project director, Orlando Burke, I suspect.'

'Sounds like a film star,' says Panos.

'He'd make a better film star than archaeologist, that's for sure. He's a crony of Koutalas. Rumour has it that Koutalas only put up the money for the dig on condition that he could select the project leader himself. Philistines,' he hisses angrily.

Liam seems to be getting gloomier and gloomier. Maybe that's what comes of spending your life digging around in ruins.

'What will happen to the treasure, if you find it?' you ask. 'Do you get some kind of reward?'

Liam gives you a withering look. 'Of course not. There's no *financial* reward in it for me. Anyway, it's now impossible to take antiquities out of Greece.'

'Unless you smuggle them out and sell them to a private collector with no questions asked, yes?' says Panos.

Both you and Liam are rather taken aback by this sudden display of knowledge.

'Yes. But that would be highly illegal, wouldn't it?' replies Liam ambiguously.

Panos yawns. 'Come on, let's go back.'

On the journey down to Simnos, Liam's remarks linger in your mind.

Turn to **47**

4

Feeling a bit shy at first, you move cautiously into the crowd and start dancing. Soon your nervousness fades away as you begin to enjoy yourself. Penny and her friends are close by – no one really seems to be dancing with anyone. The DJ, a tall, black guy in baggy khaki trousers and a string vest, keeps the tempo up and the heat rises. Eventually, just as you think you can't take any more, he changes to a slow, smoochy number. People around you start to pair off. What will you do?

Return to your table   Turn to **86**
Ask the DJ for a request   Turn to **310**

5

5

'Sure, I can teach you to windsurf,' Panos answers with a smile.

'How much is it a lesson?'

He screws up his face as if he is making a difficult calculation. 'A dance.'

'A dance?'

'A dance at the Black Cat tonight.'

You shrug off his suggestion and insist that you intend to pay the standard rate like everyone else, but Panos will not hear of it. 'You work with Penny at the villa, yes?' You nod the affirmative. 'Well, the villa brings me good custom. And besides, I like to teach you.'

Before you can react, a shout from along the beach alerts you both to the fact there are customers waiting for lessons.

'I must go, my brother calls me. Don't forget that dance.'

You watch Panos jog away to tend to his business, unaware that you yourself are also the subject of someone's scrutiny. From the beach bar, a dark girl of about your own age has been observing your conversation. Her expression is not friendly.

Gathering up your belongings you make for the village with your shopping list.

Turn to **63**

6

You realize that you have been a bit brutal but it is too late to take back those words. You have hurt him. You don't want to lose him as a friend, so you apologize in your turn.

'Friends, then,' he says with a smile.

'Friends,' you agree.

Turn to **66**

7

Matt goes to kiss you but something makes you turn away from him. Your mind is brimming with questions about the things you have heard and seen on the yacht.

Do you want to share your discoveries with Matt?

Yes   Turn to **331**
No   Turn to **47**

8

Very carefully, you close the door without shutting it completely and stand with your ear glued to the crack. Even so, you find it extremely difficult to hear much of the conversation, since Garth Craigmillar is talking quite quietly. You can only catch the occasional words . . .

'Matt Jardine's up at the windmill . . . we need to be careful . . . lot of money . . . is it worth the risk? . . .'

Intrigued, you are determined to try to hear more and ease the door open a fraction. Unfortunately, at that moment, the door is caught by a gust from the open window and it springs open, far wider than you had intended. Garth Craigmillar swings round at the sudden noise and sees you standing there, clearly listening. His face suddenly goes hard and, with a swift movement, he slams the door in your face.

Deeply shocked and embarrassed, you decide not to risk going outside again until he has gone. When you hear the door of the annexe slam after him, you nip outside to the corridor and have a look at the phone book. Sure enough, Garth Craigmillar has recorded an international call of ten minutes and left a 1,000-drachma note to pay for it. International call, but was it to the States as he claimed? There's no way of telling and so you decide to go to bed.

Turn to 320

9

You find Liam immersed in a highly detailed conversation with one of the other students on the dig. With some difficulty, you attract his attention and draw him to one side, out of earshot. He is not pleased to hear that you want to leave.

'But I can't go now!' he protests. 'We're reaching a crucial phase on this section and I have to be here to work on it.'

You are almost tempted to tell Liam about the things you have seen and heard but then you think better of it. Perhaps it would be best not to trust anyone who has connections with the dig. You bid him farewell and cajole one of the young boys lounging around by the jetty into rowing you back to the mainland. .

The rest of the day passes in a haze and your mind is full of the strange happenings on Simnaki.

Turn to 346

10

You decide to leave the guests to their own devices and settle down to making plans for the following day. A thorough sort-out in the kitchen seems a good place to start and you spend a profitable hour checking through the cupboards and making a huge shopping list.

This task done, you have to decide what you want to do next. You're quite tired – it has been a long day – and there will be a lot to get done tomorrow.

If you decide to call it a day
 and go to bed   Turn to **236**

If you decide to stay up a
 bit longer   Turn to **174**

11

The stone gives suddenly beneath your hand and falls from the wall. You screech in horror and disgust at the half-chewed, embalmed skull which leers down at you from its resting-place of centuries. Protruding from the eye socket is the muzzle of a rat, huge and grey and quivering. Disturbed from its nibblings it scurries out through a hole gnawed in the top of the skull and flees in terror. The skull rocks gently on its shelf and, still grinning, topples slowly towards you.

Turn to **109**

12

Your knee lands bang on target and Boris lets out an agonized yell. As he doubles up in pain, you clench your fists together and bring them down hard on the back of his neck. He slumps to the ground and lies there groaning.

You hear a footstep behind you and whirl round to discover who's creeping up on you. To your amazement, it is the writer, Matt Jardine. Before you have time to speak, Matt rushes to Boris's side and tries to haul him to his feet.

'Get up, you idiot! Get up! You've got to get back to the yacht!'

Groaning and cursing, Boris staggers to his feet and stumbles off down the alley. You shrink back into a doorway as he passes. Matt stares after him for a moment, fury blazing in his eyes, before he turns to you, schooling his features into a more normal expression.

'That must have been a nasty experience for you,' he says sympathetically. 'Boris is an animal. But he's faithful to his master, Koutalas. He's taking a message back to the yacht for me and it's vitally important that he doesn't miss the launch.' He pauses and then continues, 'We're planning something special for Koutalas's birthday next week. I wouldn't like it to go wrong because of Boris's stupidity.'

He seems to wait for a reaction from you and seems relieved when you say something non-committal. As an explanation for his extraordinary behaviour, it seems rather weak to you.

Matt escorts you back to the waterfront, half-heartedly offers you a drink, which you refuse, and then leaves you to walk home on your own.

Turn to 324

13

Quickly distancing yourself from the typewriter, you stand in the centre of the room, and brace yourself for Matt's entrance. The wooden door is kicked open with a bang and your unsuspecting host struggles in with two heavy plastic jerry cans full of fresh water drawn from the village well. When he sees you he stops dead in his tracks and his features betray deep annoyance.

'Perhaps you would like to tell me what the hell you are doing in here?' he demands in a nasty voice, his customary laid-back expression now distorted in anger.

You decide there is only one way you are going to get out of this one . . .

What did you do last night?

If you walked along the cliff
path   Turn to **27**
If you stayed in or went to
the disco   Turn to **157**

14

The shopkeeper seems extremely pleased that you have bought the pendant, explaining that it was made by her disabled son, Yanni, and that the symbol is an ancient sign of Aphrodite and is supposed to bring great fortune. You are happy to have bought something which has a link with the island and the goddess who seems to have played such a large part in its history, as well as bringing pleasure to the shopkeeper. Add 1 Luck point.

Turn to **188**

15

As luck would have it you do know a bit about motorbikes, having had a succession of bike-mad boyfriends in the past. Many a Saturday have you spent in damp garages holding cans of engine degreaser and oily rags. A rapid survey of the damage tells you that you are going to need some spare parts. Abandoning Panos to his private grief, you set off purposefully to the village you passed about a kilometre back where there was a garage. When you arrive there, the garage with its solitary, old-fashioned pump looks pretty deserted. As you are nosing around the yard, an old woman dressed in black, wearing an apron, pops her head out of the bungalow next door. 'Dimitri – *fagito* now – *theka* minutes.'

From this extraordinary mixture of Greek and English you deduce that the garage attendant, Dimitri, is now having his lunch, and will be back in ten minutes. Fair enough. Why not treat yourself to an ice-cold Coke, while you wait?

All in all, it is a good hour before you have your missing part and can rejoin Panos.

Turn to 53

16

It's a long wait. You have almost given up hope by the time you hear the pop-popping of Liam's bike returning. He apologizes for failing to notice that you weren't still following him and you explain the problem. His face falls.

'I don't know the first thing about bikes,' he says, 'but I'll have a go.' You watch sceptically as he starts fiddling with the moped.

Are the Fates with you? Throw a die.

1–3	Turn to 262
4–6	Turn to 148

17

For a few seconds you remain immobile, outstaring each other. It looks as if this initially unpleasant encounter could develop into something exciting. Matt may be rather too full of himself, but he's certainly much more interesting than any of the boys back home – including Nigel. Matt places his hands on your shoulders and you both move fractionally closer.

BANG. BANG. BANG. A loud rapping like gunfire makes you both jump apart. Swivelling round in fright you see a figure peering through the half-open shutters.

Turn to 283

18

Luckily, you are quite a good rider, having worked some holidays in a stables. Donkeys are quite a different matter, of course, and riding side-saddle doesn't help, but at least you manage to duck the low-hanging olive branches as the donkey careers on at breakneck speed. Eventually, you manage to get the creature under control and turn it to walk slowly back up through the grove.

Liam and Angelis, both visibly shaken, have run after you and you meet them on the way up. Angelis gives vent to a torrent of Greek and gesticulations, while Liam asks you gently whether you are OK. You reassure him and ask for a translation of Angelis's diatribe. Liam blushes and then hastily says it is all too fast for him. You throw him a suspicious look but he won't say any more.

You all agree to have several hard words with the rider of the motorbike if you meet him again.

After a short rest to calm yourselves and the animals, you set off again for the old town.

Turn to **198**

19

The author of those trashy novels you found lying around at Matt's place! So Rex Vitulli is actually staying somewhere on Simnos. As you are leaving the Post Office who should you collide with but Matt. The two of you exchange a rather stilted hello. When Matt emerges from the Post Office some minutes later he finds you still dawdling outside reading Nigel's letter.

'Looks like some pretty interesting news,' he remarks at the look of absorption on your face. You hurriedly fold up the letter.

'N . . . no, not really,' you stutter. Feeling at a momentary loss for words you inquire whether his visit to the Post Office was fruitful. This is merely an attempt at polite conversation, since you have just sifted through the contents of the Post Restante box, and you know full well that there were no letters addressed in his name. To your surprise he pats his breast pocket and says: 'Yeah, a couple of business letters from home – nothing exciting.'

Do you:

Quiz him on this statement?   Turn to **167**
Let it go?   Turn to **323**

20

Neither Garth nor Liam join you, both managing to convey the impression that they think discos are a rather childish amusement. Feeling a bit peeved, you wander off with Penny to the disco, where you have a rather dull time. None of her friends are there, and you don't recognize anybody either. The young Greek DJ on tonight has a dreary taste in music. Eventually, you give it up and wander home to bed at a much earlier hour than either of you had expected.

Turn to **324**

21

'I've got some sea-urchin spines stuck in my foot. They aren't poisonous, are they?'

Panos smiles reassuringly. 'No, they are not poisonous, but they may become infected if you leave them. Come, let me see.' With the precision of a surgeon Panos prises out the remains of the spines from your foot.

'You English girls, you come out to Greece, you have no idea of the dangers that await you.'

'What do you mean?' you ask, choosing to ignore the obvious dual meaning in Panos's words.

'Why, I mean things like the *akhinos* – a sea urchin as you call it. Very dangerous.' He releases your ankle from his firm grip. 'Now you can dance all night at the disco without pain.'

Do you:

Take the opportunity to inquire about windsurfing lessons?	Turn to 5
Offer to buy Panos a drink at the beach bar to thank him for his kindness?	Turn to 37

22

Just as you are leaving to find Liam, the dreaded Donna Chadwick makes an appearance. She has a long and involved complaint about the state of her mother's room to make. You don't like Donna, though her mother, Irene, has always been pleasant to you. When you can get a word in edgeways, you explain to Donna that cleaning Irene Chadwick's room was one of Penny's chores this morning. Donna refuses to listen and demands that you follow her upstairs to inspect the room. She seems determined to make a full-scale row out of the issue. What do you do?

Repeat that it's Penny's problem	Turn to 204
Give in and follow her upstairs	Turn to 84

This remark elicits a derisory guffaw from Matt. 'A friend . . . a friend,' he mimics. 'My dear girl, how *can* you be so naïve. Don't you know by now that for an English girl to be just "friends" with a Greek man is about as likely as a vulture making friends with its prey – and I think you'll find Panos Pavlides just about as typical as you can get . . . Little Greek girlfriend tucked away out of sight, leaving him free to flirt with all the tourists . . . yes, he's got it all worked out.'

'You sound as if you're quite envious of him, Matt!'

Matt shakes his head and gives you a patronizing pat on the shoulder. 'Keep deluding yourself, honey. But don't come running to me if Panos Pavlides turns out to be too hot to handle!'

You are relieved to see Penny making her way along the road towards you. She is ecstatic because the elusive Garth Craigmillar has asked her to accompany him to a reception the following day on board the *Hera*, Georgios Koutalas's sumptuous yacht which for the past few weeks has been moored outside Simnos harbour.

Matt does little to disguise his lack of interest in Penny's prattlings. He says he has got work to do and disappears, leaving you to accompany her on a tour of the boutiques to hunt out something suitable to wear for the party.

Turn to 251

24

Liam gives you a disappointed look. He considers going down the tunnel on his own but then chickens out, confessing that he's not too keen on enclosed dark places. He says he'll have a go next time he comes up here with one of the other students on the dig.

Turn to **182**

25

You make it quite clear to Donna that Villalink will not be prepared to cover any additional hotel bills incurred by the Chadwicks, or anyone else, and suggest that if she has any complaints about the accommodation she should communicate them immediately to head office. The firmness of your voice appears to have taken the wind out of Donna's sails for a moment. Explaining that you must now see to the needs of the other guests, you make a hasty exit down the corridor. Something tells you that your triumph over Donna is only to be a temporary one. It looks like she's going to be a tricky customer.

Where do you go from here?

Out on to the balcony for a
   breath of air to calm yourself   Turn to **103**
Back to your bedroom   Turn to **287**

26

All of a sudden, his face changes. All the friendliness disappears in a flash, leaving behind a new Garth, one with granite features and hard, unsmiling eyes. But try as you might, you can get no satisfactory reaction from him. He doesn't go as far as suggesting that you must have imagined the whole episode, but you feel that this is implied. It is only when he hands you out on to the jetty at the other end that he says anything remotely helpful.

'About that business on the island – I should forget it, if I were you. It could be dangerous for you to get involved. Just leave it alone.' And so saying, he stalks off without another word. Maddening!

You make your way back to the villa alone and get through the rest of the day somehow, though your thoughts are in turmoil. Eventually, you make your exhausted way to bed.

27

Mustering a relaxed smile, you shrug nonchalantly:

'I suppose I just wanted to see you.'

Matt drops the jerry cans with a thud on the stone floor, and strides purposefully over to you.

'You seem to be under the misapprehension, honey, that it's open house up here . . . The truth is, I have elected to live in this rather shabby hermitage because, you know what I value above everything else in life?'

You shake your head mutely.

'I value privacy. And that means a definite *no* to uninvited guests.'

He pauses and moves closer until his disarming cobalt blue eyes are only inches from your face: 'Even if they are of the attractive, female variety . . .'

Do you:

Stand still?	Turn to 17
Move away?	Turn to 185

28

You have a long wait, which is eventually rewarded by the sight of a dark, shadowy figure leaving the hut and making its way down the little path to the secret *tholos*. You decide to follow at a safe distance.

Turn to 116

29

Silence.

'Well, you might at least say you're sorry,' you snap, trying not to notice how handsome he is. Panos surveys the damage for an instant, then winks and hurries off dragging the windsurfer sail behind him.

Typical, you think, a half-wit. He obviously didn't understand a word! You shake out your towel and lie down again, angrily brushing some of the sand off your sticky body.

'Here . . . something to wash this nasty sand out of your mouth.'

You open one eye. A bottle of ice-cold lemonade

is poised about two inches above your nose, proffered by a brown hand with a silver identity bracelet. You'd love a nice long cool drink.

Do you:

Refuse the drink and turn your head away?	Turn to **123**
Take the bottle?	Turn to **61**

30

Back at the party, you find Penny standing rather disconsolately on her own. She doesn't appear to be enjoying it as much as she had expected: deserted first by Garth, then by Matt. You too feel a bit out on a limb, so when Garth reappears, you tell him that you have both decided to go home. He looks a little surprised but accepts that you have to get back to the villa. You catch the next launch back and spend the rest of the afternoon on the beach, windsurfing and sunbathing. Around tea-time, you make your way back to your villa.

Turn to **47**

31

You feel you ought to let Matt know that you are going exploring with Liam, but he appears to have done a vanishing act. Perhaps he is hiding out in the site hut. You peep around the door.

'Excuse me, I was . . .' the sentence dies on your lips as you are confronted with the sight of Garth deep in conversation with a girl not much older than yourself who is lovingly cleaning a morsel of ceramic with a cloth.

'Garth, I didn't realize *you* were here today.'

'Oh, Garth is a regular visitor,' smiles the girl, barely looking up from her work. You are surprised to feel a flicker of jealousy.

'Er – yes, I occasionally come out here to get away from it all,' adds Garth, a shade too quickly.

You ask if either of them has seen Matt recently.

'I saw him about ten minutes ago,' answers the girl. 'He was heading off towards the other side of the island.'

'Probably in search of inspiration,' suggests Garth, with a note of scorn in his voice. 'You know what these writers are like – they just "vant to be alone",' he mimics, in his best Greta Garbo voice.

Well, if Matt has abandoned you, you might as well take Liam up on his offer. You head back to the temple to find him.

Turn to 105

Next morning, in the narrow galley kitchen, Penny is moping about trying to make sense of the packed-lunch requests. She squints at you through eyes puffy with the remains of last night's mascara.

'Rather overdid it at the Black Cat,' she groans. 'Feel awful.'

Together you lay the trestle table and set out the continental breakfast: freshly baked bread, just delivered by Yanni the baker, dark yellow honey, and rich goat's milk yoghurt. Anxious to avoid Donna Chadwick you nip into the kitchen for a snatched cup of coffee.

Penny sighs and clutches her head dramatically. 'I must lie down or I won't make it through the day. You couldn't be a real star and cope with the shopping alone this morning, could you? You know where everything is now.'

You reassure Penny that you can manage and quickly compile a list of ingredients for the evening meal, plus a few basic stores that need replenishing. Throwing on a long T-shirt over your bikini, you grab a large straw basket and step out into the bright sunshine.

Do you:

Decide to take a detour via the beach?	Turn to **225**
Decide to take a detour via the windmill?	Turn to **49**
Decide to take a detour via the Villa Xanthi?	Turn to **94**

33

Matt gives a knowing smile. 'It's OK, honey, I'm quite tame. But if the thought of entering the lair of a wild American, unchaperoned and at night, makes you nervous, why don't you stroll up and pay me a visit sometime tomorrow evening?'

Do you:

Take Matt up on his original
offer of a drink to prove you
are not afraid?   Turn to **177**

Make a vague promise to visit
Matt the next day and return
to the villa?   Turn to **320**

34

You discover that you are resting against a sharp piece of rock and gently begin to saw away at the tape that binds your wrists. Eventually, the tape parts, you free your ankles and, at the next available moment, make a run for it.

Turn to **256**

'You aren't being very sociable tonight,' observes Garth Craigmillar with mock reproach, having discovered you sitting alone on the wall outside the Black Cat disco. You explain that you are debating whether to turn in and get an early night in preparation for your exciting assignment tomorrow. However, when Garth hears that you are to be Matt's guest aboard Koutalas's yacht, he seems faintly uneasy.

'What do you know about Matt that I don't?' you ask crossly.

'Nothing exactly,' answers Garth with reluctance. 'Listen, it's just a hunch I've got that perhaps Matt Jardine isn't the sort of person you should be getting involved with. You can tell me it's none of my business of course. Matt calls himself a writer, but when does he have time to write? He spends his days lounging around in bars, making a show of "fraternizing with the natives", and hanging about with some pretty strange people . . . Oh well, you're a sensible girl. I'm sure you can take care of yourself.'

You respect Garth's judgement but feel annoyed at him for trying to ruin your outing. Seconds later a screech of brakes interrupts your solitary confusion. Panos jumps off his beaten-up Vespa and comes over to you. You decline his invitation to dance, explaining that you are tired and need to be left alone for a while. But persistence is Panos's middle name.

'So, tonight you are tired. But tomorrow you have a free day?'

You nod warily.

'I too am free tomorrow. Perhaps we two could make a little excursion. We could go high up into the mountains, there is an old, old monastery there, Aghios Dionysus, full of strange stories and legends. I could show you some of the mountain villages where tourists never go . . . What do you say?'

Well, what *do* you say?

That you have a prior engagement? Turn to **161**
That you will meet Panos at
    midday on the harbour   Turn to **221**

36

He listens carefully and then laughs as you reach the end of your breathless tale.

'And you thought we were planning some high skulduggery! I can't wait to tell Burke. This'll really dent his self-esteem, being cast as the villain of the piece! There's nothing illegal happening on the island,' he says, his voice becoming deep and sincere. 'We haven't publicized the discovery of the secret tomb, since there are just a couple of dubious characters working on the dig and we want to be sure that *all* the treasure reaches the right people.' He takes your chin in his right hand and turns your face up to his. 'You do believe me, don't you?'

Well, do you?

Yes   Turn to **128**
No   Turn to **152**

37

'How come you speak such good English?' you ask.

'Through talking with the tourist girls,' he replies gravely . . . then winks at your disapproving look. 'No – I am joking of course. I have returned only this season from your country. I was working in a restaurant in London for a year. I managed to save up enough to buy all the equipment I needed to start up the windsurfing school.'

'How much does it cost for a lesson? I've always wanted to have a go.'

'For you, *mikra mou*, nothing . . . Come on, do not look so suspicious. The Villa To Limani brings me good custom. Besides, it would give me pleasure to teach you.'

He rocks forward on his chair and places his hand on top of yours on the table. You withdraw your hand quickly as you catch the eye of a girl standing on the steps leading up from the beach. Her dark complexion and simple dress tell you she is a native of the island. Her look of obvious displeasure tells you she is also connected in some way with Panos, who springs up from the table.

'Ah, excuse me. I must go.' He hovers for an instant before taking his leave, and says meaningfully, 'I am often in the Black Cat in the evenings.'

Not sure whether this parting remark is a statement or an invitation, you wait until Panos has disappeared before returning to the beach to collect your belongings and setting off for the shops.

Turn to **63**

38

Penny claps her hands with pleasure and immediately plunges into a detailed conversation with you about the clothes you two are going to wear. Garth smiles gently before excusing himself and returning to his own table. Out of the corner of your eye, you can see that Liam has relapsed into silent contemplation of his beer. You feel a twinge of guilt and then dismiss it, but wonder whether Liam doesn't have something else on his mind.

Eventually, when the clothes topic has been exhausted, you and Penny make your way to the Black Cat, leaving Liam still sitting there.

'Funny boy, that,' Penny remarks as you leave the waterfront. 'Always in a dream, never listens and he's awfully dull. He was worse than usual this evening. Really seemed to have something on his mind, didn't you think?'

You make some non-committal remark, but find yourself wondering just what it could be. He seemed so keen to take you up to the old town, and yet he hardly knows you.

You have a rather dull time at the disco. None of Penny's friends are there and you don't recognize anybody. The young Greek DJ on tonight has a dreary taste in music and you give it up, wandering home to bed at a much earlier hour than either of you had expected.

Turn to 324

You walk down a long corridor, trying to find a cabin that distinguishes itself as a bathroom. After a few minutes you select a door at random and gingerly push it open. You enter a sumptuous bedroom with a bathroom *en suite*. You cannot resist having a quick snoop. A dressing-table with a gilt mirror and a set of ivory hairbrushes. Various bits of expensive bric-à-brac. A bookshelf well stocked with holiday reading – Alistair Maclean, a few Maigret novels, a couple of Greek paperbacks, and a whole series of detective novels by a writer called Rex Vitulli. You take one of these books down from the shelf. Scribbled in the front is a message to Koutalas in bold, loopy handwriting: 'To many future ventures, and future successes! Very truly yours, R.'

You replace the book and go into the bathroom to attend to your dress, musing over your find. A few seconds later, you hear the door to the bedroom being opened.

Do you:

Come out of the bathroom to see who it is?	Turn to 87
Freeze and hope they don't discover you?	Turn to 95

40

You struggle but to no avail. He is immensely strong. You fill your lungs and are about to give vent to an ear-shattering scream, when a voice suddenly hisses behind you. 'Don't be an idiot, Boris! This is no time to be fooling about. You've got to get back to the yacht with that message. Georgios will flay you alive if you foul up now!'

Boris drops you without a second thought and pushes roughly past you to head back up the alleyway. You look up, hoping to be able to thank your rescuer but are astonished to discover that he has disappeared! A glance up an alleyway to your right gives you a glimpse of a fair-haired man hurrying away, but in the night-time gloom it is impossible to identify him. You have a feeling that the voice was somehow familiar, but you can't place it. Feeling very shaken, you make your way cautiously down to the waterfront and then back to the villa, pondering on this strange encounter.

Turn to **324**

41

Panos jumps to his feet defensively. *'Ti kanis etho?'* he asks – a question you recognize from your phrase-book browsings, meaning 'What are you doing here?'

These words release a torrent of angry recriminations from the girl, who casts frequent looks of displeasure in your direction. Your presence seems to be adding fuel to her argument . . . Better make yourself scarce before a full-scale row develops. You scoop up your belongings and, in an artificially jolly tone, explain that you must get on with your chores.

Panos turns to you apologetically: 'I'm sorry. I have to go. My mother is asking for me to help her at the hotel. She has sent a friend to fetch me.'

His 'friend' does not appear to understand English, but glowers on silently.

Not at all convinced by this rather weak excuse, you leave them to their own devices. Hopefully Panos will not forget about the promised boat trip to the island.

Turn to 63

42

The journey home is swift but uneventful. Even so, it is later than you had planned by the time you get back to town, so you leave Liam to return the mopeds to the hire shop and head for home.

Turn to 47

43

Matt stalks up to where you are sitting with Liam and whisks you away to introduce you to some new people he has met during the party.

Come early evening you are beginning to feel you have had enough and ask Matt to arrange for the launch to take you both back to the jetty. Matt is in high spirits after an afternoon's diet of champagne and compliments from admiring fans. He places his hand on your shoulder.

'Glad you came?' he asks softly.

'Yes,' you reply without hesitation.

Why have you replied 'yes' to Matt's question?

Because you find him an intriguing
    and attractive personality and
    would like to spend more time
    in his company   Turn to **169**

Because you have accumulated
    some interesting information
    during the course of the
    afternoon   Turn to **7**

44

Deciding that you shouldn't really leave a stranger to roam free in the annexe, you hover outside until Garth has finished. Eventually, he emerges and tells you that he has left a 1,000-drachma note by the phone, which should cover his call, according to the charges posted on the wall.

Much to your delight he stays chatting for a while. You find yourself warming to this man and wonder whether you can contrive to meet him again.

However, before you can work the conversation around to this, Garth rather abruptly takes his leave of you, and leaps over the small white fence surrounding the villa's garden before striding off down the path towards his own villa. You console yourself with the thought that you might be able to arrange to see him tomorrow. You toy with the idea of checking up on your guests and then decide that you have had enough of Donna Chadwick for one day and go to bed.

Turn to **320**

45

Footsteps running along the passage fill you with sudden panic. Where will you hide? You crouch in a crevice in the crumbling masonry and cover your face with your arms. Perhaps it's all a ghastly nightmare. The glare of a powerful torch confirms this is not so. Squinting into the darkness you see a shadowy face looking down at you. A face usually relaxed and smiling, now twisted in fury.

Turn to **279**

46

Boris seems to find your attempt to hurt him amusing.

'Naughty! Little kittens shouldn't show their claws! That's not nice!' So saying, his mouth descends on yours. A shudder runs through you as his wet lips slobber over you, but there is nothing you can do about it. After a few moments, he lets you go, smacks you on the behind and shoos you off down the alley, promising to continue the next time you meet. For a moment you seriously consider trying to stand your ground and hurl abuse at him but then, wisely, you decide that discretion is the better part of valour and beat a hasty retreat.

You walk back to the villa in a rage. Lose 1 Luck point.

Turn to **324**

47

Tonight you slump into bed thankfully, only to find that your mind is much too active to enable you to sleep. Even the chirping of the crickets in the undergrowth and the rustle of the cypress trees seem to have lost their hypnotic powers this evening. Eventually you sit bolt upright and impatiently turn on the light. You feel hot and bothered and your head has begun to ache. You fetch a glass of water from the bathroom and scrabble around in your handbag for an aspirin. Nigel's two airmail letters stare up at you reproachfully amidst the debris of old bus tickets and tubes of make-up. Guiltily you realize that in all the excitement you have barely skimmed through the first letter and completely neglected to read the second. You go back to bed and read his first letter again.

Turn to **121**

48

You walk down a long corridor, trying to find a door that distinguishes itself as a bathroom. After a few minutes, you select a door at random and gingerly push it open. A sumptuous bedroom, but with a bathroom *en suite*. You cannot help having a quick snoop. A dressing-table with a gilt mirror and a set of ivory hairbrushes. Various bits of expensive bric-à-brac. A bookshelf well stacked with holiday reading – Alistair Maclean, a few Maigret novels, a couple of Greek paperbacks, and a whole series of detective novels by a writer called Rex Vitulli. You take one of these books down from the shelf. Scribbled on the front is a message to Koutalas in bold, loopy handwriting: 'To many future ventures, and future successes! Very truly yours, R.'

The handwriting looks familiar. Very familiar. Then, suddenly you remember. It's Matt Jardine's handwriting. You've just seen him sign one of his own books and the handwriting was identical. What could this mean?

You replace the book and go into the bathroom musing over your find. A few seconds later, you hear the door to the bedroom being opened. You start guiltily. What do you do?

Come out and see who it is	Turn to **190**
Stay put and hope not to be discovered	Turn to **318**

The whitewashed walls of the mill are cracked and peeling, its sails now static and prey to the ravages of the wind. An ideal hideaway for a writer . . . no visitor without a definite purpose would want to undertake the climb. Tentatively you knock on the door. No one at home. Absent-mindedly you give the rusty latch a sharp tug and the doors creak open to reveal a cluttered den with crude cooking facilities. The internal machinery has been removed to make way for a raised sleeping platform. You make a swift mental inventory of the contents of the room: stacks of yellowing copies of the *New York Times*, a collection of dog-eared paperbacks thrown higgledy-piggledy into a tea-chest, a half-eaten meal which is acting as host to a colony of flies, a desk with a scratched portable typewriter . . . Casting a guilty glance over your shoulder, you walk over to the machine and examine the piece of paper protruding from the roller: 'McGrath drew his Colt and cocked the safety-catch. He was taking no chances. "Tell me or I'll flatten you," his voice rasped like a . . .'

'Hm, some literary genius,' you remark cynically to yourself. 'Still, what can you expect if he takes his inspiration from trash like this.'

At the side of the typewriter lies a collection of luridly jacketed detective novels: '*Johnny Rio and the Dimestore Murders* by Rex Vitulli, *Johnny Rio and the Vegas Diamond* by Rex Vitulli . . . He certainly seems a fan of this Rex Vitulli character . . . Still, I suppose even literary geniuses must relax sometimes . . .'

At that moment a dog barks outside and you hear the put-put of a moped engine. Matt must have returned. You have a feeling he is not going to be pleased to see you. Do you:

Stand your ground and rely on
your charm to get yourself out
of a tricky situation?   Turn to **13**
Escape through an open window?   Turn to **59**

50

There's a rather nasty moment as Penny makes it clear that she doesn't see why she should cover for you. You bite back the hot retort about having covered for her, as you would rather not have Garth and Liam witness an unpleasant argument. It's embarrassing enough as it is. You turn to Liam and apologize, and suggest another date, making the suggestion possibly rather more warm than you would normally have intended. Liam visibly brightens, Garth looks openly amused, Penny triumphant. You suddenly feel sick of the lot of them.

'So you can come to the yacht tomorrow, then,' Penny tells you.

Will you go, or will you refuse, paying Penny back for her uncharitableness?

Agree   Turn to **38**
Refuse   Turn to **90**

51

You promise Donna that you will report her complaint to head office and see what can be done (knowing full well that Villalink are not going to pay any extra hotel bills run up by the Chadwicks, or anyone else). Mumbling something about 'lots to do in the kitchen' you scurry off down the corridor leaving Steve, Donna's long-suffering husband, and her mother Irene to pour oil on troubled waters. You sense that this isn't going to be the last you hear from Donna – perhaps you shouldn't have been so feeble?

As you round the corner the sound of a loose shutter banging in the wind makes you start. The noise is coming from Room 9. The door is ajar. Should you:

Walk in?	Turn to 85
Ignore it and go and look for Penny?	Turn to 103

Liam suddenly remembers that his key-ring has a tiny torch on it and snaps it on. Its feeble light doesn't have much impact on the gloom ahead of you but at least you can now see the ground beneath your feet. Eventually, the tunnel opens up into a small round chamber, with no visible exit from it other than the way you came. The air is still and musty, but breathable. You realize that this chamber may well have been a hideaway for someone in troubled times, a kind of ancient priest's hole.

Liam edges cautiously round the room, using his torch to probe the darkness and then turns his attention to the walls. With a cry of astonishment, he calls you over to the wall he is inspecting.

At first, the marks thrown out by Liam's little torch mean nothing to you, and then they suddenly click into place. It's a map. An ancient map!

'I can't be sure, but I think this is a map of the temple that we're excavating at the moment!' He traces the outlines with his fingers. 'Here's the antechamber, this is the main altar room and this . . . this must be one of the *tholos* tombs, I guess. You can see it's marked with the sacred symbol of the goddess. That's where the treasure, if there is any, should be.' He turns to you and you can see his eyes glinting with excitement. 'I'll get the lads up here tomorrow and we'll take photographs. What a find! What a discovery! I'll be famous!' He turns back to the map.

Just then you hear something that makes your blood run cold. A voice at the top of the tunnel and the glimmer of torch-light. Your instincts tell you that it would be better not to be found down here and so you grab Liam, gesture to him to keep quiet and the pair of you creep into the little further chamber. With Liam's torch switched off, you might just escape notice.

It seems an age before anything happens, during which you try to keep your breath shallow and under control, both because of the stench in your hiding-place and also for fear of being discovered. Eventually, two shadowy figures enter the main chamber and flash their torches around. The map of the temple is soon revealed and it is clear that this is what they're after. Then, to your shock, one of them begins attacking the map with a small pick-axe. In moments, the map will be ruined! You feel Liam stiffen beside you.

Are the Fates with you? Throw a die.

1–3   Turn to **70**
4–6   Turn to **176**

Now you have patched up the scooter sufficiently for you to continue your journey, you decide to restore your flagging spirits with a couple of ice-creams. With all this stopping and starting it's well after three o'clock when you get your first glimpse of the monastery, but you have to admit that it has been well worth waiting for. Built on the summit of the highest peak on the whole of the island, it rises majestically to meet the sky, like a huge white domed Christmas cake. Basking serenely in the afternoon sunlight Aghios Dionysus appears a place of concord and tranquillity. Only its wide battlements and the 300-step stone staircase leading to the main gates testify to its stormy past, when the monasteries of Greece were repositories of great wealth, and plundering hoards sailed the Mediterranean.

After an exhausting climb you are greeted at the gates by a black-robed, bearded monk.

'Welcome, young people, welcome to the monastery of Aghios Dionysus,' he says in Greek. Panos translates for you and you nod and smile in response.

'Ah, the young lady is English,' exclaims the monk, delighted to have the opportunity to demonstrate his knowledge of the language. He introduces himself as Adelfos Yannis Theologos, Brother John the Evangelist, and offers to show you around. You'd really rather explore on your own, but it would be impolite to refuse. Brother John ushers you into the main chapel and spends five minutes pointing out the beauty of its many gold icons depicting the lives of the Saints.

'When was the monastery built?' you ask, anxious to show interest.

'This particular edifice was constructed mainly during the fifteenth and sixteenth centuries,' he replies. 'But there has always been a holy building on this site. It is the highest pinnacle of the island, and therefore, in the eyes of our forefathers, nearest to God. In pagan times there was a temple here in honour of Eros, Aphrodite's winged servant, and over the centuries relics, found at the Sanctuary on Simnaki, have been brought here for safe-keeping. We have built up a fine little collection of artefacts in our museum here. Nothing of great value of course, since they have only just begun this year to excavate the site seriously.'

The hollow chimes of a bell resonate throughout the chapel.

'Ah, it is time for devotions. Excuse me. Feel free to look around. Before the war when I joined the order, there were over a hundred monks here. Now we are but twenty. We enjoy receiving visitors from the outside.'

With a rustle of black serge he is gone.

'What a talker!' laughs Panos. 'Still I suppose it must be a lonely life up here. I've had enough history for today. I'm going to admire the view.'

Do you want to follow Panos?

Yes	Turn to **81**
No	Turn to **239**

54

As luck would have it, you discover that the collar of
the wetsuit has been mended with a small piece of
waterproof sticky tape. You unpeel this carefully
and stick it over the tiny but deadly hole in the
dinghy. A makeshift mend but it might hold for a
while . . .

A day and a half later, you are found by a passing
fishing boat. You are weak and suffering from expo-
sure but at least you are alive. The fishermen are
very kind, wrap you up warmly and give you bran-
dy, while they tell you of the horrifying vandalism
and theft of treasure from the temple of Simnaki.
Ruefully, you reflect that had you been a bit wiser
and a lot luckier, this story might have had a different ending . . .

Lose 2 Luck points. Check your score at the back
of the book and try again!

55

After an initial, rather shaky start, you manage to
get nearly everything on your shopping list. You are
relieved to discover that most of the shops Penny
had pointed you towards have at least one person
who can speak reasonable English, though you
notice that your fumbling attempts at asking for
things in Greek are greeted with great enthusiasm
and encouragement. You resolve to keep up with
the language as it is clear that your efforts are
appreciated. Who knows? A smattering of Greek
might well turn out to be useful.

Laden with your heavy shopping, you decide to

take the bus back to the To Limani inlet, rather than trying to walk it. The sun is beginning to beat down with a baking heat on your unprotected head and, on an impulse, you dive into one of the beachfront tourist shops in search of a suitable straw hat.

In the cool of the shop, you pause, your eye caught by the unusually attractive display of island curios. Would you like to buy something as well as the hat?

A pendant with a strange symbol
on it   Turn to 14
A small icon   Turn to 110
None of these   Turn to 96

56

It all sounds very attractive, but it will mean deserting your job with Villalink, something you don't really want to do. You thank Garth kindly and, since there seems little more to say, go off alone to find Penny.

Turn to 30

57

'Matt Jardine, the famous writer,' sneers Panos. 'You should not let yourself become involved with this man.'

'You talk as if there is some sort of rivalry between you.'

'Rivalry? I would not waste my time,' he snorts, all traces of amusement gone from his voice.

You press him to throw some light on his warning but he clams up and refuses to volunteer any more information. You look for a change of subject.

'I like the scooter, Panos, is it new?'

Panos's expression lightens.

'Yes, you like her? I bought her only last week. Perhaps you would like to come for a ride. I am going to Paleopoli to deliver something to my uncle's farm. We can be back this evening.'

You explain that you have to be back in time to help Penny prepare supper, but add that the following day is your day off.

Panos looks delighted.

'Ah, in that case, perhaps tomorrow we can make a little excursion? Have you been to the monastery of Aghios Dionysus? No? It is a fabulous place, full of strange stories and legends. There are also many mountain villages that you should see.'

Panos arranges to pick you up tomorrow by the harbour wall at midday.

Turn to 127

58

Unfortunately, you haven't the foggiest idea where to start. It doesn't seem to be anything obvious and, by the sound of things, you are in danger of draining the battery if you go on trying to start the engine. You'll have to wait for Liam.

Turn to **16**

59

The only escape route that is immediately apparent is a small window – you wrench open the shutters and hover momentarily on the window ledge. It must be at least a ten-foot drop on to the ground below.

Are the Fates with you? Throw a die.

1–3	Turn to **271**
4–6	Turn to **329**

60

Liam explains that the old town of Castro is four or five miles away as the crow flies but that it will probably be at least a couple of hours' walk, since the only way to get there is across the hills along donkey-tracks. He suggests that you either hire a moped each, or go with a guide on donkeys. Which will you choose?

Mopeds	Turn to **242**
Donkeys	Turn to **268**

61

The lemonade is wonderfully refreshing. You gulp it down greedily. Panos sits down beside you on the sand and introduces himself.

'A very crafty peace offering,' you observe, draining the bottle.

'You English are so stern,' jokes Panos. 'I thought if I stayed to apologize you might try to bite off my head . . .'

If you want to take this opportunity to ask Panos about windsurfing lessons	Turn to 5
If you feel this inquiry might sound too much like a chat-up line	Turn to 107

62

Your swift reactions save you – at least for the moment. You dodge past the man plodding heavily up the path, catching him by surprise. However, the four of them are now on to you and running down the path behind you. As you reach the top of the cliffs above the beach, you turn and realize with horror that they are gaining on you. There is no way that you will be able to reach the beach before they catch you if you stick to the path. What will you do?

Hide	Turn to 156
Give up and wait	Turn to 102
Jump into the sea below	Turn to 194

63

Your errands completed, you begin the arduous trek homewards with several bulging carrier bags. You are just passing Nikos Taverna with its blaring *bouzouki* music when without warning the handles of your heaviest bag give way, sending a cascade of tomatoes, onions and miscellaneous household items down the hill. As you grovel around on the path in a frantic attempt to save the rest of your shopping, a white jeep pulls up beside you.

Smiling down at you is a strongly built, russet-haired man, probably in his late twenties, with pleasant regular features, and an amused twinkle in his eye. It's Garth Craigmillar. He gets out and picks up a couple of very dusty tomatoes.

'Yours, I think. Here, allow me,' he offers, taking hold of your bags and reloading the weight more evently. 'Which way are you going?'

You reply that you are heading for To Limani.

'I'm going that way. Let me give you a lift.' He loads your shopping into the back of the jeep and drives you up the hill. When you reach the villa, he deposits your bags on the front doorstep.

'Perhaps we'll meet again, since we're neighbours,' you venture hopefully.

'Yes, quite likely,' comes the brisk answer, dashing your immediate hopes of an invitation to the Villa Xanthi for a neighbourly cup of coffee. With a brief smile and a wave he is gone. His arrival at the adjacent villa is signalled shortly afterwards by the noise of savage barking. So Penny was accurate in her assessment – Garth Craigmillar is obviously a man who likes to keep himself to himself.

Turn to **91**

64

When you reach the waterfront, Penny suggests having a drink or two in a bar, since the disco prices tend to be very high. You are happy to be guided by her and follow her along the waterfront looking for an empty table.

Suddenly, Penny sees a sandy-haired stranger sitting on his own nursing a bottle of beer and she drags you over to meet him.

'This is Liam MacNamara,' she says, introducing you. 'You remember, I told you he's the one who's interested in the history of Simnos. He's always grubbing around looking for broken pottery bits out by the old town, and he's full of stories about the island's past. Last time, I remember he told me a fascinating story about the legendary treasure of Aphrodite, which is supposed to have disappeared on the little island.' She turns to Liam, laughing. 'Have you found it yet?'

Liam doesn't appear to find Penny all that amusing and you begin to get the feeling that she is deliberately teasing him. He seems nice enough, thin-boned, wearing clothes that seem to have been bought for his height, rather than his width, and hang very loosely on his spare frame. His dark-brown eyes are sharp and intelligent, though with sandy eyelashes matching his hair, he looks vaguely vulnerable at the same time. You decide that he could look attractive when he smiles but that on the whole his is the kind of face you remember for its character rather than its looks.

Apart from the dig on Simnaki, Liam's current obsession seems to be an old ruined fort up in the hills at Castro. While Penny is chatting to Garth Craigmillar at another table, Liam offers to take you up to Castro tomorrow. You are intrigued by the sound of the old fort. You'd like to take a genuine ancient Greek souvenir home. And yet you do have to think about your work, since a day's jaunt with Liam will mean asking Penny to cover for you. What will your answer be?

You'd like to go, but you'll
   have to talk to Penny first   Turn to 224
You can't go   Turn to 126

65

Apprehensively you tear open Nigel's letter and stroll out into the sunlight.

'A letter from your boyfriend in England, yes?'

You look up and see Panos grinning at your startled expression. Embarrassed, you swiftly fold up the letter and cram it into your bag. Do you:

Admit the letter is from Nigel?	Turn to **119**
Say the letter is from your mother?	Turn to **187**

66

He helps you to your feet and supports you as you walk gingerly back up to the path where the other two donkeys wait patiently. Eventually, Angelis comes back leading your runaway donkey. After a brief conversation with him, Liam turns to you anxiously.

'How are you feeling? Do you want to continue, or are you too shaken up?'

What will you do?

Go home	Turn to **172**
Go on	Turn to **198**

'Why did you get mixed up in all this, Matt?' you ask, as he unties you.

'I had no choice really,' he answers wearily. 'I guess that where you come from getting on the wrong side of the law seems a pretty bad thing. Where I'm from it's more like a hazard of everyday life.' He pauses. 'When I started writing I never dreamed what fame and fortune lay ahead of me. You see, where I come from making it big meant moving three blocks up town and having enough cash to get to the end of the week without having to borrow – or steal – to eat. I worked my way through college and wrote in the evenings. When my first novel was accepted I couldn't believe it. When it started selling I thought I must be dreaming. And then I started gambling. Having tasted wealth I was crazy for more. This seemed like an easy way of getting it. The trouble was, the more successful I became as a gambler, the worse I became as a writer. It began taking over my whole life. My day was spent waiting for the gaming tables to open. I stopped writing eventually. Well, apart from some trashy detective stories to keep body and soul together.'

'Under the pseudonym of Rex Vitulli?'

'Actually it's not a pseudonym, Rex Vitulli is my real name. Not quite as classy as Matt Jardine, eh?'

You bid him continue, mesmerized by this confession.

'That was when I met Koutalas. He baled me out of one or two real bad scrapes. I owed money all

over. He persuaded me to come in on this with him.
I say "persuaded". You can imagine how "persua-
sive" a man with Koutalas's wealth can be, with
henchmen like Boris at his command . . . Koutalas
had a tip-off that there was treasure on this island.
He promised to pay off my debts and said there
would be plenty more besides. Seemed like a good
idea at the time . . .'

How would you describe Matt after his confession?

A weak character who has cast his
   lot in with a load of villains,
   and who is now trying to blame
   his background for the mess
   he is in   Turn to **183**
The victim of a disadvantaged
   upbringing whose search for
   financial security has led
   him into bad ways   Turn to **171**

You find Garth Craigmillar a bit of a mystery. For some reason he seemed keen for you to visit Koutalas's yacht tomorrow, but now, walking along the dusty road towards the inlet he doesn't have much to say for himself. After a few false starts, which only produce monosyllabic replies from your companion, you ask him about Koutalas. To your surprise Garth becomes alarmingly serious.

'Georgios Koutalas is a very dangerous man. He's up to his neck in all sorts of shady deals and is known not to balk at violence to achieve his aims. But he's also very, very clever. The police forces of at least three countries would give a lot to be able to pin something on him, but so far he's proved too slippery for them.'

You gasp with astonishment and ask rather breathlessly why Garth seems to be so friendly with Koutalas, if he's such a villain.

'It's very simple. His import/export company is a client of ours. We spend a lot of Koutalas's money laundering his company's image and making it acceptable to the Great British Public. But I don't know how much longer we'll be doing it. Things seem to be stirring in his company and I get the impression that there will be rather weightier problems than publicity to worry about in the near future.' He laughs and turns to you. 'Anyway, Koutalas does give very good parties! Why don't you change your mind and come too?'

He reaches out and strokes your cheek gently. A friendly gesture, but one that sends an unexpected spark shooting through your body. The shock of pleasure leaves you speechless for a moment, while Garth smiles down at you, his dark eyes fixing yours, moonlight glinting in his hair. The warm night scent of thyme mingles with the aromatic presence of the olive groves and rises with the distant tang of sea air and, in that moment, you and he are the only two people alive.

Then suddenly the spell breaks as a nearby dog barks a warning to some imaginary intruders, Garth's hand falls from your face, and you turn to continue your walk up the hill.

'I mean it,' he says. 'I'd like you to come to the yacht tomorrow.'

Would you like to go?

Yes	Turn to **286**
No	Turn to **274**

69

Panos is in a bit of a mood with you for being so unhelpful and doesn't seem inclined to believe your story.

'Perhaps you fell asleep in the heat and dreamed it,' he says dismissively.

You have to admit the incident was pretty strange. After all, what was a man dressed in a white suit doing, running around up here in the mountains, miles from anywhere? Probably a complete nutcase, you tell yourself. Anyway, for the moment, the mystery will have to remain unsolved.

Turn to **53**

70

Before you can stop him, Liam rushes forward with
an angry cry. Taken by surprise, the two vandals are
at a disadvantage and Liam gets in one lucky blow,
which knocks the man with the pick-axe to the
ground, where he stays, unmoving. But then Liam
gets locked in an unequal struggle with the other,
much bigger man. It's only a matter of moments
before he gets seriously hurt. What will you do?

Rush into the fray   Turn to **108**
Stay where you are   Turn to **168**

71

You find Garth taking detailed snaps of the dig with
his little pocket Olympus. He seems quite happy to
leave when you suggest it. Once you are on the little
launch back to the main island, he turns to you and
asks whether you are all right.

'You're looking flushed and bothered. Did anything happen back there?'

You look into his friendly brown eyes and see
nothing there to alarm you, but remember that you
don't know all that much about the mysterious Mr
Craigmillar. Will you trust him and tell him everything, or will you keep quiet?

Tell him   Turn to **26**
Don't tell him   Turn to **238**

72

You catch him by surprise and make a clean escape. For a moment, it looks as though he might follow you and make a scene, but one of his mates catches his arm and says something urgently to him. Boris's group leave soon afterwards and you make your way over to the little stage.

Turn to **310**

73

The atmosphere at the Black Cat tonight is exuberant. Jason, the West Indian DJ, is entertaining the crowd with his famed breakdance routine. You look on, mesmerized by his suppleness and agility. You feel a tap on your shoulder and swivel round to meet Panos's coal-black eyes. He bids you follow him.

Outside on the terrace you slump against the wooden railings and inhale the scent of the sea and lemon groves.

'Perhaps you and I could make a little excursion tomorrow, then? We could go up into the mountains and visit the monastery of Aghios Dionysus. A very strange place, full of legends – and a few mad old monks! What do you say?'

A tempting way to spend your free day. You arrange to meet Panos the following morning at midday by the harbour.

The walk up the hill to To Limani seems to get steeper every day. As you near the villa, red-faced and panting, you notice the shadow of a man sitting

on the terrace smoking a cigarette. It's most unusual for any of the guests to be up and about at this time of night. You feel a shiver of apprehension.

'Hi!' says Matt Jardine.

'You nearly gave me a heart attack,' you gasp accusingly.

'I've been waiting for you for nearly an hour. I thought I'd come and make my peace. I've come to invite you to a party.'

'What party would that be?' you inquire warily.

'It's on Koutalas's yacht, the *Hera*. Don't look at me as if I'm half crazed. It's a genuine invitation. If you're interested in taking me up on it, be on the jetty at midday. There'll be a motor launch to pick us up.'

Two invitations in one night – which will you accept?

Matt's invitation	Turn to **161**
Panos's invitation	Turn to **221**

74

The journey home is slow and uneventful. By the time you get back to town, you are feeling very saddle-weary and are not looking forward to having to prepare the evening meal. Leaving Liam to settle up with Angelis, you head back to the villa.

Turn to **47**

The stone slab resolutely refuses to move. Centuries of grime have sealed it fast to its resting-place.

'Ah well,' sighs Liam resignedly. 'There was probably nothing there anyway. All the other tombs have had their treasures plundered and I doubt that this one would have proved the exception to the rule. Still, we'll have to come back at some stage with the proper tools just to make sure. It would be ironic if the only one we didn't examine thoroughly was the one that housed the statue.'

'Statue?' you ask, blinking in the sunlight as you emerge from the sombre depths of the beehive tomb.

Liam explains that this Sanctuary was reputed to have been the home of a fabulous gold and ivory effigy of the goddess Aphrodite by the famous Greek sculptor, Praxiteles – one of the greatest craftsmen of the ancient world. You are just getting interested in this story when a young woman struggling with a wheelbarrow full of earth calls Liam over to give a hand. Liam excuses himself and rushes to her assistance.

Have you had enough of ruins for one day?

Yes   Turn to **293**
No   Turn to **269**

76

The effect on Burke is electrifying. The little stove crashes over, papers fly everywhere, and Burke himself dives for the door, grabbing a gun from a shoulder holster as he runs. Within seconds he is round your side of the hut, with the nasty little gun pointing unwaveringly at your midriff.

'Oho! A snooper, eh? Well, you'll soon find out what we do to snoopers!' he snarls.

Turn to 138

77

You must have gone about 300 metres from the main temple in a westerly direction when you reach a dead end. Blocking your chosen route is an inhospitable barbed-wire fence with a large sign slung across it:

DANGER   KEEP OUT
UNSAFE GROUND

Your curiosity aroused, you peer over the fence to try to see what is so dangerous. The path looks perfectly OK to you. Do you want to continue?

Yes   Turn to 309
No   Turn to 293

78

Silently, you dress, making sure that your clothes are all black and that you have soft shoes on your feet. You creep out of the villa and head for the rendezvous with Liam. Together, you make your way down to the jetty. You had planned to steal one of the little boats that cluster there during the day, so you are dismayed to discover that most of them have gone. The ones that remain have been disabled, or had their oars taken away – a natural precaution taken by their owners. Lose 1 Luck point. You look despairingly out towards the island; it's much too far to swim and the currents in the channel between the islands are known to be treacherous. Suddenly, you are struck by a brilliant thought. The windsurfers!

You lead Liam down to the beach and over to Panos's store hut. It is locked, of course, but you remember seeing where he hid the key the last time you were there. You are in luck and the key is there.

As you drag one of the sailboards out, you notice that Liam has become strangely silent. You ask him what the matter is.

'Um . . . well, you see . . .' He sounds embarrassed. 'I never . . . I can't windsurf. I've never used one of these things!'

This is a serious blow. You have few doubts about your ability to reach the island but to have to teach Liam would take up far more time than you have. You'll have to leave him behind.

In only a few minutes you are ready. The board is fixed up and you are kitted out in one of Panos's black wetsuits. You carry the board down to the sea, launch it, set the sail and head out to sea.

Are the Fates with you? Throw a die.

1–3   Turn to 92
4–6   Turn to 186

The cheerful coloured sail of a windsurfer veers towards you.

'Right arm straight . . . Lean back . . . *Careful!*'

Oblivious to the directions issued from the shore, the windsurfer continues to wobble precariously, finishing up in a spectacular capsize a few feet from where you are swimming. The issuer of the instructions wades into the water to help his pupil who is floundering with the sail.

'No, no, no, Philippe,' he laughs. 'Still, I think perhaps we make some progress today, yes?'

As the instructor is helping to pull the board on to the beach you float nonchalantly on your stomach and take a sidelong glance shoreward. Sleek, tanned skin, lazy dark eyes, a mass of tight curly hair . . . 'I know who you are,' you say to yourself. 'You're the notorious Panos.' Do you:

Pluck up courage to go and ask about windsurfing lessons?	Turn to **5**
Swim on to the nearby rocks to observe Panos from a safe distance?	Turn to **195**

80

Your gentle knocking goes unnoticed for a while. But then Burke stiffens with suspicion and turns towards the window. However, you are too quick for him and have ducked out of sight. He resumes his work, shaking his head in a puzzled fashion. You knock again, this time accompanying it with an eerie, rising moan. Within seconds, Burke is out of the hut snooping around. But again you are too quick for him and have hidden before he reaches the place where you were. Burke wastes several minutes staring into the shadows around the hut and although you are alarmed to see that he carries a gun, you are pleased to observe that the hand that carries it is extremely shaky. Burke then returns to the hut and you begin your ghostly campaign again, only this time, ending a series of knocks and moans with a blood-curdling shriek.

Are the Fates with you? Throw a die.

1–3   Turn to 296
4–6   Turn to 180

81

'Oh, oh, it's Liam,' groans Panos.

Sitting on the battlements is the archaeology student – he's dressed in frayed khaki army shorts several sizes too big and a faded University of Cambridge T-shirt.

Panos tries to steer you away.

'No, it's mean. Anyway, he's seen us,' you protest.

'Oh well,' says Panos. 'I suppose there's not much wrong with him.'

General opinion of Liam is that his mind seems to be trapped in a time warp that ends around AD 200. But he looks pleased to see you both. He says the dig was beginning to get him down so he decided to take a day's holiday.

'Do you come here a lot?' asks Panos.

'Whenever I get the chance. I suppose I'm always on the look-out for clues.'

'Clues?' you and Panos repeat in unison.

Turn to **3**

82
Are the Fates with you? Throw a die.

1–3	Turn to **12**
4–6	Turn to **46**

83
Your chosen path takes you around the perimeter of the island. You shudder as you look down into the angry sea below with spray flying from the jagged rocks. Eventually the track peters out and your way is obstructed by thick gorse and bramble. There's nothing of interest here to make you battle your way through. Better return to base.

Turn to **293**

84

Irene Chadwick's room looks immaculate to you, but Donna moves around it, finding fault all over the place. What do you do?

Tell her she's being unreasonable
and leave her   Turn to 288
Follow her around, giving the
room another clean   Turn to 326

85

Lingering for a moment by the open window of Room 9, you look out across the courtyard. There's Penny, topping up her tan, clad in the barest of bikinis, lazing on a sunlounger. Her piercing laughter wafts back to you. She's absorbed in conversation with a stranger – an eccentric-looking young man in his early twenties, dressed in a garish Hawaiian beach shirt and baggy cotton trousers. He is deeply tanned, but obviously not immune to the heat from the way he is mopping his brow on his sleeve. Without warning he looks up to the window where you are standing. Embarrassed, you make a show of fiddling with the catch of the shutter and slam it closed. You make your way to the kitchen, and start to peel the potatoes for supper. Annoyingly, the face of this good-looking young man refuses to be banished from your mind. Maybe there will be a chance to get to know him better?

Turn to 299

86

You sit nursing your lukewarm Coke for a while, watching the dancers gyrate round the floor. There is a particularly noisy group of men on a table not far from you. They seem a bit out of place in the disco, as they are rather older than most of the people here, and dressed in everyday jeans and T-shirts, rather than disco clothes. Although they seem to be drinking heavily and intent on having a riotous time, they don't look like normal tourists. As you watch them, you become aware that one of the group is eyeing you up and down. He's a large rather unattractive man with a beer-belly flopping over the top of his over-tight jeans, and a distinctive tattoo of a serpent snaking up his arm. As soon as you notice his attention, you look away, but it is too late. With a word to his mates, he eases himself out of his chair and makes his way over to you.

'Would you like to dance?' he asks.

But when you refuse politely, he just sits himself beside you, places a sweaty hand on your knee and clearly intends to stick with you. What will you do?

Stick it out, hoping Penny will
    return to rescue you   Turn to **106**
Brush past him, making some
    excuse   Turn to **246**

87

'Garth!'

'I thought I spotted you dashing in here. Everything OK?'

'I'll know what they mean next time I hear the term "luxury yacht",' you observe drily, indicating the opulence around you.

'Hmm, may well be the last flowering before the decay sets in. Rather like the last days of the Manchu dynasty . . . their most glorious moment was achieved just at the point of decline.'

You ask him what he is driving at, but it is apparent that he feels he has been a trifle indiscreet and wishes to curtail the conversation. 'I daresay we'd better venture back into the fray . . . I'm sure there would be a terrific scandal if we were discovered together in one of the cabins!'

What will you do?

Go back and join the party	Turn to **189**
Tell Garth you want to have another stab at removing the wine stain from your dress	Turn to **339**

88

You like Garth a lot, but not that much. After a few minutes' pleasant conversation, you excuse yourself, saying that you should find Penny.

Turn to **30**

When you peer at the stone more closely you see that it bears the symbol of Aphrodite, an emblem which you have spotted many times in its diverse forms throughout the last few weeks. You give the stone a tug. To your surprise it comes away in your hands – someone has obviously been here before you. Shining your flashlight into the dark hole you feel your jaw drop in amazement. There, in a chamber no more than six feet square, is a treasure trove that would put the tomb of Tutankhamun to shame. Gold masks, caskets full of heavy gold bracelets and necklaces, earrings and pendants of fine filigree work, drinking vessels ornamented with the heads of golden rams and dolphins, cases full of chunky gold coins, amulets and daggers, small statues cast in bronze, all sealed in for centuries and preserved virtually intact.

But on a ledge carved into the stone, stands the most breathtaking treasure of all – the form of a beautiful woman, modelled in gold and ivory. You have found the legendary statue of Aphrodite. Gain 2 Luck points.

You pull yourself together and replace the stone. Better get out of here before you are discovered. Perhaps you should keep this to yourself until you can decide on the best course of action.

Who did you come to the island with?

Matt	Turn to **97**
Garth	Turn to **71**
Penny	Turn to **191**
Liam	Turn to **146**

90

'Oh well, be like that then,' says Penny crossly. 'We'll be thinking of you tomorrow night as we're dancing out on the bay.'

'I'm sorry that you won't be able to come tomorrow,' Garth smiles, 'but perhaps you'd like to come another time. Old Koutalas is a very social animal and I'm sure I'll be invited again. You could come then.'

You thank Garth and then, before you can say any more, Penny makes a move to go to the Black Cat. Will you go with her as planned, or would you rather make an excuse, saying you need to write a letter home, and go back to the villa?

Go to the Black Cat   Turn to **20**
Go to the villa   Turn to **264**

91

Once you have established your daily routine the days fly past. Even with breakfast and supper to prepare, beds to make and provisions to fetch from the town, you are still left with a fair amount of free time. Often, after you have washed up the evening meal, you and Penny find yourselves heading for the bright lights of the Black Cat disco, a popular night-spot, to meet friends and dance to the latest sounds. Nor has your dancing been confined to the disco variety. The regulars at Nikos Bar have undertaken to teach you the *sirtaki*, a traditional Greek folk dance at which you have become surprisingly proficient.

With daily lessons from Panos, by now you have

grasped the rudiments of windsurfing. You can't deny that Panos is an excellent teacher, but on a personal level your relationship is less satisfactory. It is difficult to tell whether he is really interested in you, and whether his attentions are sincere. Matt Jardine is another one it's difficult to fathom. On the few occasions you have met him, he has always been proved to be good company, if rather arrogant. On the other hand, he has a moody side to his character which you find disturbing. The person you would really like to get to know is Garth, but he seems intent on keeping to himself. The only evidence of his comings and goings is the occasional barking of the dogs at the gate of the Villa Xanthi.

As you begin to make your own circle of friends and acquaintances you find you are spending less time tagging along behind Penny, whose latest project is to get in with a crowd of students (mostly male) who are working on the archaeological dig on the small offshore island of Simnaki, excavating the ruined Temple of the goddess Aphrodite.

One night Penny returns from the Black Cat in a state of great agitation.

'Had a good evening?' you ask.

'Fantastic! I got chatting to one of the archaeologists working over on Simnaki – a shy Irish boy called Liam. He told me there's a possibility of hidden treasure on the little island. We must go over there one day and check it out!'

You agree this sounds like an exciting project for one of your free days.

Decision-making is becoming increasingly difficult in this hot, languorous land, where the philosophy of *avrio* – that is, putting off until tomorrow what you should do today – dominates every area of activity. After only a short time on the island you can well understand why buildings lie unfinished, why buses fail to arrive on time, and why a substantial crisis may elicit no more than a resigned shrug. This just isn't the climate for efficiency.

Turn to **147**

92

It is a clear, moonlit night and the island stands stark black against a silvery shimmer of the sea. There is a fresh breeze and your progress is good. However, just as you leave the bay and head out across the strait, a sharp gust of wind catches your sail, almost ripping your arms out of their sockets. The tide is running against you and you struggle desperately to control the sailboard.

Are the Fates with you? Throw a die.

1–3	Turn to **136**
4–6	Turn to **328**

As the small launch bobs its way to the island of Simnaki the talk is mainly about the technicalities of the excavations.

You ask Liam why the director of operations is not travelling out on the launch with his team.

'Oh, he's probably skiving off again this morning. He usually turns up around midday for a few hours.'

His comment sparks off a chorus of complaints from the others.

'He's never around when he should be.'

'Frightened of getting his hands dirty.'

'Struts around in his immaculate white suit whilst we do all the spade work.'

You infer from these remarks that the director appointed by Georgios Koutalas, Orlando Burke, is not blessed with the unquestioning loyalty of his workers. Gazing up at the sheer rockface of the island, you ask Liam how on earth you are going to get to the top of the cliffs.

'Relax, there's an inlet and a path round the far side. You won't be required to scale the rocks!' he laughs.

As you round the nugget of land the ruined pillars of the marble temple become visible.

'It's quite breathtaking,' you murmur, drinking in the view.

'It would be a lot more breathtaking if we found the treasure,' mutters Liam bitterly.

Turn to **241**

94

The other villa on the inlet looks charming as you approach it along the narrow path etched out between the gorse and the wild thyme which covers the otherwise bare headland.

The morning sun beats hotly on the back of your neck and you realize that unless you are quick, you are likely to have to toil back up the hill, laden with shopping, in the heat of the noonday sun. Still you intended to visit the little villa, and visit it you will.

There's no sign of life and as you walk briskly down the path towards the villa, you become increasingly sure that the place is deserted. Suddenly a furious barking breaks out and two large black dogs hurtle out of the shade on the veranda and bar the path in front of you. They look vicious. What will you do?

Turn back and go shopping   Turn to 55
Try to make friends with the
    dogs   Turn to 154

95

You hold your breath whilst the intruder pads around the cabin. After less than a minute the clicking of the door signals his retreat. It was probably just another guest who had lost his way.

Turn to 339

96

After some consideration, you decide that most of the objects on display have very little real value and are no more than mere souvenirs for tourists. You decide to buy the hat.

Turn to **188**

97

You can't find Matt anywhere and are just about to give him up altogether when he suddenly material-izes from behind a pillar. You start, guiltily, and he looks at you with suspicion hardening in his eyes. Hastily, you suggest going back to the mainland and Matt agrees.

It's only when you are half-way across the narrow channel, which separates the two islands, that Matt turns and asks you the question you have been expecting.

'Something happened to you back there. You're looking all hot and bothered. Want to tell me about it?'

He is standing very close to you, gazing intently at your face. You feel sure that he will be able to tell if you lie to him. What will you do?

Tell him the truth	Turn to **36**
Make something up	Turn to **308**

98

You rejoin Jason and spend a pleasant time watching him work. He actually becomes quite relaxed and chatty and you start talking about music and other general things. He tells you quite a bit about Liam too. Apparently he has quite a bee in his bonnet about the ancient legend of the missing treasure of Simnos. This all sounds quite interesting and when Liam reappears, you ask him about it and are rather surprised when he seems to be a bit evasive. Eventually, Penny finds you and suggests that you both make your way back to the villa.

Turn to 320

99

With a firm flick of the throttle the scooter takes off along the dusty road, making a noise vaguely akin to a swarm of enraged bumble-bees. You have no choice but to clutch Panos tightly round the waist. Rounding a sharp bend, Panos swerves to avoid a man strolling along at the side of the road. As you zip past, you realize that it is Matt Jardine that you have narrowly avoided squashing against the wall of the Pension Acropol. You shout an apology back at him, but your words are obliterated by Panos's deliberate revving of the engine. A few moments later you hit a flat stretch and Panos reduces his speed.

'You know that man?' he asks.

'Who? Matt? Yes, slightly,' you admit.

'It would be better for you that you do not know him at all,' replies your companion surlily.

Is Panos being prematurely possessive, or is he giving you some kind of warning? Your questions will have to wait because the thrumming of the engine makes any reasonable discussion impossible.

Turn to **137**

The donkey's frenzied rush takes you straight amongst the olive trees. Within seconds a low-hanging branch sweeps you from the saddle and you land with a sickening thud on the hard stony ground. Your mount gallops off into the distance. Liam hurries to your side, while Angelis pursues his disappearing donkey, cursing volubly in Greek.

Dazed, you open your eyes to see Liam looking anxiously down at you.

'Don't move! Lie there and get your breath back. Have you hurt anything?'

You test your limbs gingerly and are relieved to discover that you have got off with a scare and some bruises. Liam produces a handkerchief and some water and offers to sponge your forehead. Would you like this?

Yes   Turn to **214**
No   Turn to **66**

101

WRONG! You were hoping this ledge would lead to a secret hiding-place, but there appears to be nothing unusual here. Lose 1 Luck point.

Turn to 45

102

They catch you and bundle you roughly down to the beach where their launch is now waiting. Bound hand and foot, you are left helpless in the main cabin while they unload the rest of the treasure. Your heart sinks as you contemplate the various possible Fates that may lie in wait for you. Your chances don't seem to be very good.

Turn to 260

103

The strident peal of Penny's laughter wafts up to the balcony. Squinting across the sunbaked courtyard with its borders of parched red and pink geraniums, you spot her – bikini-clad and recumbent on a sunlounger. She is giggling up at an eccentric-looking young man dressed in baggy cotton trousers and a gaudy Hawaiian beach shirt. You are too far away to tell what they are saying, but whatever the gist of his conversation, this handsome stranger seems to have a rapt audience in Penny. As he talks he assumes a theatrical air, waving his hands expansively, and occasionally thrusting back a stray lock of sandy hair from his eyes. You go to call out, but sensing your interruption might not be welcome, stop short. There is something rather unusual about this unkempt young man. He doesn't have the look of a tourist about him, yet he is clearly not a native of the island. Still, this is no time to daydream – it's past six o'clock and there is supper to prepare. Retiring to the narrow galley kitchen you start to attack a huge mound of unpeeled potatoes.

Turn to 299

104
If you don't make a guess, you'll have to head back to the villa and miss your afternoon on the yacht. Do you want to guess?

Hermes and Zeus	Turn to 340
Apollo and Hermes	Turn to 244
Apollo and Icarus	Turn to 162
Go home instead	Turn to 312

105
'The classical temple you see before you was constructed around 400 BC. The reason it is so fragmented is due to the fact that this part of the Aegean was subject to a great deal of seismic instability during this period.'

'What?' you reply.

'Earthquakes,' explains Liam condescendingly. 'This island is actually built of volcanic rock. That's why the earth is so fertile, and why the artefacts we have found are so well preserved.'

'You mean we are actually standing on a volcano?' you inquire with alarm.

'A long-since extinct volcano, yes. You can rest easy though, it's unlikely that it will spring into action again after over two thousand years.'

You follow Liam obediently away from the temple towards the cliffs.

'Now the temple built in classical times actually stands on the site of a much older edifice dating back to the great Mycenaean age. The interesting thing about the people of this period is their way of burying the dead. Which brings me to my surprise.'

You find yourself standing before the entrance to a dark tunnel. You ask Liam where it leads.

'It leads to a *tholos* tomb,' answers Liam excitedly. 'We have found a circle of ten such tombs on this island, as is the usual pattern. The wonderful thing about these particular burial chambers is that they were so economical spacewise. The bodies were shoved into the tomb, with all their armaments and treasures, and when it was needed again, the tomb was reopened, the existing skeletons moved to one side, and more bodies buried alongside.' Failing to notice your growing disquiet, he concludes with a crestfallen sigh, 'Only this time we haven't found any treasure. It must have been plundered by pirates, or Egyptians, or Saracens – at any rate, it's not there . . . Would you like to see inside?'

Well, would you?

Yes	Turn to **163**
No	Turn to **265**

106

He edges closer to you on the bench, so that you can feel his hot breath on your cheek. He tries to impress you with a lot of talk about how he works on the big yacht anchored out in the bay, which belongs to the shipping millionaire, Georgios Koutalas. The way he talks, you'd be forgiven for thinking that he virtually runs the boat single-handed. He is drinking steadily, his voice is getting thicker and thicker and he keeps squeezing your leg. You see Penny on the dance floor and desperately try to send silent signals to her, but she doesn't appear to see these. Your companion, who urges to you to call him Boris, is really becoming a pain. What will you do?

Try to discourage him politely   Turn to **220**
Brush past him, making some
  excuse   Turn to **246**

The ice is now broken and you fall naturally into conversation. On a one-to-one basis Panos drops his guise of super-confident beach Romeo and chats unaffectedly about himself. After some minutes there is a lull in the conversation. Panos points out to sea.

'She is beautiful, yes?' He sighs wistfully.

You look up fully expecting to behold a bronzed goddess on a surfboard, but see no one.

'Simnaki . . . the island of Aphrodite,' he continues. You agree that in the radiant sunlight the small nugget of rock across the strait looks very attractive. You ask Panos if it is inhabited.

He shakes his head. 'Once they used to take the sheep there for grazing, but now there are fewer sheep and more *thermokeepia* – greenhouses – on the mainland, and there is enough pasture. Today the small island is only inhabited by birds and rabbits – and the archaeologists who have come to dig in the ruins. I will take you there if you like. I have a small boat. You know, there is a very strange story . . .'

He stops in mid-sentence. A slight dark-haired girl of about your own age is stalking determinedly across the beach. Her destination appears to be the spot where you and Panos are sitting. Do you:

Withdraw tactfully?	Turn to **181**
Stay and see what she wants?	Turn to **41**

108

You grab a small rock and dash to Liam's aid. Surprise is on your side and you manage to fell the big man before he has time to realize what is happening. You go over to Liam, who's clearly stunned but appears to be recovering. You turn your attention to the map again, hoping to find something quickly before the two vandals regain consciousness. Your luck is in. You see another *tholos* symbol, some distance to the west of the main temple.

Gain 2 Luck points.

A groan behind you reminds you that there is no time to lose. You grab the pick-axe in the vain hope of preventing any further damage to the valuable map, collect the still woozy Liam and dash for the exit.

'What do we do now?' You turn to Liam anxiously. He looks worried.

'Don't say a word about this to anybody,' he replies in a low, urgent voice. 'Those were no ordinary vandals. I reckon we've stumbled on something big!'

'But shouldn't we tell the police?'

'What for? The map's beyond rescue now. They wouldn't do anything – and we've no proof.'

You decide to go home. How did you get to Castro?

By donkey   Turn to 74
By moped   Turn to 42

109

When you come to you are lying on a coarse blanket in the dazzling sunlight. A crowd of concerned faces look down at you. Liam is anxiously sponging your forehead.

'You fainted,' he explains apologetically. 'Sorry about the skull. He must have been some sort of weird offering to placate the goddess. We hadn't got around to examining that tomb yet. Nasty shock if you're not accustomed to that sort of thing.'

You try to sit up and groan. There appears to be a large egg-shaped lump on the back of your head.

'Better take the young lady home,' says a dapper grey-haired man in a white suit. You recognize him as Orlando Burke, the director of excavations. As you are carried down the mountain path by two strapping Swedes, you have a feeling that you might be missing out on an exciting day.

Turn to 254

110

Unfortunately, the icon is a fake and is not even worth the money you have spent on it. Still, you are happy to have something that is Greek, even if it is very modern Greek, and you plan to hang it on your bedroom wall.

Turn to 188

Gnarled fig trees, stunted by lack of moisture and the hot sun, flank the uneven donkey track which meanders around the headland. In the daytime there is a fair bit of traffic along this way, mainly farmers taking a short cut to their olive groves and allotments where tomatoes and cucumbers are grown under glass. At twilight there is not a soul to be seen. After walking for some minutes, you stop to catch your breath and take in the view, savouring the peace and solitude, whilst below you the village vibrates with noise and movement. As you continue your climb round into the next bay you see a dark, craggy wedge of rock which looms out of the water about half a mile out to sea. This is the island of Simnaki – 'Little Simnos' – which in ancient times was the site of a splendid temple to Aphrodite, the goddess of Love. It appears gloomy and unwelcoming in the half-light, but perhaps in the daytime it would make an ideal secluded picnic spot? The glassy strait that separates the island from the mainland looks almost swimmable. As you stand contemplating future excursions you become aware of the laboured breathing and irregular tread of another person some way behind you. From Penny's description, you realize it's Matt Jardine, the writer. He seems lost in thought and has not noticed you yet. Do you:

Continue on your upward trail?   Turn to **255**
Make a speedy descent of the
   path?   Turn to **129**

112

Koutalas's guests seem to be a strange mix: there are the society butterflies in all their multi-coloured glory, some dark-suited businessmen talking in tight huddles, some bearded types, who can only be from the dig on the little island, and some real thuggish types, who you guess must be deck-hands. No one you know, though.

After a while, you feel a little peckish and so make your way to where the food is laid out. Unfortunately, on your way there, someone jogs your elbow and your glass of pink champagne spills down your dress creating a horribly large stain. Realizing that the dress will be ruined unless you act swiftly, you go off in search of water to sponge your dress down.

Turn to 202

113

You follow a narrow brambly path that takes you inland. A few rabbits scamper across your route and disappear again into the undergrowth, but apart from them there seem to be no signs of life and little to interest you here.

Turn to 293

114

You solve your problem by explaining that the telephone is really only for use in emergencies (getting a dig in at Donna, who has the grace to blush) and that you will have to ask him to pay for the call. Garth Craigmillar agrees and claims that he does have a real emergency.

You lead him over the annexe, resisting Donna's attempts to accompany you, and show him the phone. He picks the handle up and then pauses, looking at you. He clearly wants to be left alone. You could honour his clear wish for privacy and leave him alone, or you could retire to your bedroom, which is next door to Penny's, and try to listen to the conversation through the door. Which will you do?

Leave him alone	Turn to 44
Listen from your bedroom	Turn to 8

115

'Let's just say that it would be to your advantage to speed things up a bit.'

'It's not like digging up potatoes, you know; things have to be taken slowly. It's a delicate operation.'

'And Rex? He's a co-operative workmate?'

'He'll do. He's so desperate for cash he'll do anything we ask him.'

Your view of the two men is obscured, but from your hiding-place you can see that one of them has an unusual tattoo on his forearm, a twisting serpent inscribed in green and red inks. The conversation fades as the men move off. You wait until you feel the coast is clear and then sneak out of the cabin. Where do you go now?

Back to rejoin the party	Turn to 189
On to the deck	Turn to 155

The steep little path down to the *tholos* is even more precarious than in daylight as the moon casts shadows across the path that fool the eye. You cannot concentrate wholly on keeping your footing as every nerve is strained for sounds ahead of you. To be discovered here, on the path, at this time of the night, would be a dead giveaway. However, your luck holds and you reach the bottom of the path safely.

The little *tholos* stands in front of you, its interior bathed in a warm yellow light which streams out of the entrance. As you watch, you see a burly figure emerge with a heavy load, which he carries with great care and heads down the narrow path to the beach. Confident that your black wetsuit is excellent camouflage, you creep closer to the *tholos* and peer in. At the back of the inner chamber, you can make out two figures stooping over the entrance to the treasure chamber, reaching into it to grab hold of something that is being handed up to them. One of the men reaches up to sweep a long lock of hair back from his forehead and, seeing this familiar gesture, you realize that this can be none other than Matt Jardine! Just then, you hear footsteps approaching up the path again and you beat a hasty retreat to your former hiding-place. Unfortunately, you slip and the noise of your fall attracts their attention.

Are the Fates with you? Throw a die.

1–3	Turn to **218**
4–6	Turn to **62**

117

This is the first time you've ever seen a man hit another man in real life, and by the way Safari Suit is clutching his midriff, it seems to hurt a lot more than in the movies. You stare on, paralysed by fear, wondering what on earth the outcome of this unsavoury episode will be. Fortunately, the sight of Panos gaily striding round the bend carrying the motorbike spares sends Fat Man scurrying back to his car. When Panos arrives at the scene of the crime, he exchanges a few words with Safari Suit and helps him back into his car. Perhaps he knows this man? When the sports car has driven off, you come out of your secret lair.

'Ah, there you are,' says Panos. 'I've got the spares. Did you see that poor guy up there on the road? I find him all bent up in pain. I thought he was going to die. You know what he has? Food poisoning. Food poisoning from eating the local *kalamari* stew!' He slaps his sides, enjoying the joke.

Do you tell Panos what *really* happened?

Yes	Turn to **139**
No	Turn to **53**

118

Your walk back to the villa is a pleasant, friendly one. He opens up a lot, telling you all about the dig he's working on at the old, ruined temple of Aphrodite over on the little island. He admits to being a little mystified as to why they haven't discovered anything of much interest, since they have been working there for months, carefully scraping away each layer of earth, looking for shards of pottery or temple artefacts. You ask him about the possibility of discovering something really valuable there.

'You're talking about the island legends of buried treasure, I guess.' He looks at you quizzically. 'It would be great to find something along those lines, but, realistically, the chances are that anything of that nature would have been stolen centuries ago.'

'But, if you *did* find something like a buried treasure there, would it make you rich?' you ask.

He laughs: 'Beyond my wildest dreams! No, seriously, if we did find anything of real value there, it would belong to the Greek Government and all we'd get is a lot of thanks, *kudos*, and the chance to make a fortune by writing papers and articles about the discovery'. His face darkens. 'Though there's no doubt which of us would make the fortune. Our oh-so-eminent director, Orlando Burke. He'd make sure that nothing more than a few crumbs came our way. No, the only way I'd make a fortune would be to discover the treasure in secret and export it to a private collector, who would pay handsomely to own a beautiful, genuine temple treasure with no questions asked.' He laughs again, this time rather more grimly. 'I might even do it, at that.'

You're startled at this bitterness from someone you had thought to be so passive, and something must show on your face, as Liam quickly changes the subject.

You soon reach the villa and say goodbye.

Turn to **324**

119

Panos shakes his head disapprovingly.

'You should forget your life in England whilst you are here and try to enjoy yourself more. You know, I have a very good philosophy: Live for today and let tomorrow take care of itself.'

Is this a philosophy you agree with?

Yes   Turn to **249**
No   Turn to **217**

120

As you flop into the bottom of the boat, a horribly familiar voice welcomes you aboard. You look up and see Matt's face smiling unpleasantly at you.

'So, my little runaway. You are a slippery customer, but we've caught you now!'

You haven't a hope of escaping and you sit dejectedly at the back of the boat, under the gaze of Matt's two henchmen, as he heads back to Burke's launch. When you get there, they bind you hand and foot and lock you in the cabin.

Turn to **260**

121

14 Southfields Drive,
Lindbourne

3 July

Hallo there . . .

How are you? Terrible I bet . . . all that sand,
sun and surf – must be really getting you down!
Seriously though, I know you must be pretty
busy, what with one thing and another (?!), but I
had hoped to have received a proper letter by
now, although I did like the postcard of sunset
over Simnos.

I bumped into your sister yesterday in Sains-
bury's and she had a good moan about you not
writing. She said your mum hasn't been too well
lately, and she was making noises about asking
you to cut short your 'holiday' to come back and
help out at home. I said I didn't think you would
be too happy about that.

Well, I haven't got any more news for now,
except that I am missing you, as I'm sure you
know. Write soon.

Love,
Nigel

You still have Nigel's second letter to read, but now
you are beginning to feel decidedly drowsy. What
will you do?

Read it now   Turn to 257
Try to sleep and save it
    for later   Turn to 141

122

You stare crossly at the clock and reset it for a more normal time, before snuggling down and trying to go back to sleep. Lose 1 Luck point, for the loss of sleep.

Turn to **254**

123

Panos tuts at your stubbornness.

'Well, I leave you the bottle. Perhaps you may be thirsty later,' he says forlornly.

Oh dear. You've blown it. He seems quite a nice bloke after all. Nothing like the swaggering beach Romeo you were led to expect. Feeling despondent you head for the beach bar. Having ignored breakfast you suddenly feel peckish. You order a cheese and ham toasted sandwich and go to sit down. In a few minutes the sandwich arrives, wrapped in a paper serviette. You unfold the parcel and notice that written across one corner of the napkin is a word: S O R R Y.

Looking up with your mouth full of sandwich, you come face to face with your adversary.

'May I join you please,' he asks.

Turn to **37**

124

Are the Fates with you? Throw the die.

1–3	Turn to **232**
4–6	Turn to **58**

125

Unfortunately you don't have a flashlight with you. You try feeling your way along the passageway but it's impossible to see where you are going.

You resolve to keep mum about your various discoveries today and return to the tomb when you are better prepared.

Who did you come to the island with?

Penny	Turn to **191**
Liam	Turn to **9**
Garth	Turn to **71**
Matt	Turn to **97**

He looks disappointed and clams up again, and sits hunched in his chair, staring moodily at his beer.

Just then, Penny returns with Garth in tow and you can see that she is pleased about something.

'Garth has an invitation to join Georgios Koutalas on his yacht tomorrow afternoon and he's asked us to come too. Won't it be fun!'

'Who's this Georgios thingummy, Pen?' you ask.

'Oh, you know! The fabulously rich millionaire who owns that enormous yacht anchored out in the bay. Oh, do say you'll come! It'll be a lovely, luxurious way of spending an afternoon!'

It's true that you had noticed the yacht a few days ago and spent a few idle moments daydreaming about the kind of life its owner must lead. Here is your opportunity to find out. Garth adds his voice to Penny's invitation and you feel yourself wavering. You're aware of Liam's presence and feel uncomfortable that he should witness this exciting invitation coming so soon after his own. You worry about the guests at the villa and whether you'll be able to get back in time to cook the evening meal, but Penny pours scorn on this, saying that it won't hurt them to eat a bit later for once. What will you do?

Accept the invitation   Turn to 38
Decline because of the guests   Turn to 306
Decline because of Liam   Turn to 208

That night, as the Black Cat Disco, you come face to face with Matt Jardine. After an awkward pause he smiles at you.

'Listen, honey, you and I seem to have got on the wrong side of each other. How about us calling a truce. I've been invited to a rather special party tomorrow, and I'd like to ask you along as my guest.'

You ask him to elaborate.

'The party is actually being held on Georgios Koutalas's yacht. Don't look so sceptical! You'd be surprised at the people I know, and Koutalas happens to be quite a patron of the arts.' Spying Greg winding his way towards you with the drinks, he leans over and whispers hurriedly: 'Well, the invitation stands. If you're interested in taking it up, meet me on the jetty at midday tomorrow, Koutalas is sending a motor launch that will take us out to the yacht.'

That night in the darkness of your room you gaze out of the open shutters at the sky with its explosion of stars, and consider the options open to you. You look at the luminous dial of your clock. Midnight exactly. In twelve hours' time you will either be on your way to the monastery with Panos, or climbing into the motor boat with Matt. Which will it be?

The monastery with Panos   Turn to **221**
The yacht with Matt   Turn to **161**

128

'I thought you would,' he murmurs as he bends to kiss you. His arms tighten around you as you reach up to him and your embrace lasts until a discreet cough from the boy at the wheel draws your attention to the fact that you have reached the jetty on the mainland.

Turn to 228

129

Self-consciously you begin your descent, eyes cast determinedly downward to avoid Matt's gaze. As you draw level, he gives a jaunty mock salute and blocks your way.

'Hi! Matt Jardine,' he thrusts a sunburnt hand, adorned with what looks like an extremely expensive gold watch, towards you.

'Yes, I know. I mean . . .'

'Aha, checking up on me,' he laughs. 'Funny place for you to be walking alone at night.'

'I felt like being alone,' you answer tartly.

'Yeah, I like being alone as well. That's why I chose to make my home up here, away from the bright lights of the village. I expect you're off now to join the revellers at the Black Cat?'

'Not at all . . I was just . . .'

'Good, in that case you can do me the honour of joining me in a glass of ouzo at the mill. I'm afraid you'll find it rather dilapidated . . . but its romantic qualities make up for it . . .'

Do you want to:

Accept his offer?	Turn to 177
Decline his offer?	Turn to 33

130

Yawning, you get up and get dressed and start a normal day.

Turn to 254

131

Panos beams triumphantly at Matt's departure. It's plain to see there is no love lost between these two.

'Ah, perhaps I arrive at the wrong moment?' inquires your Greek friend leadingly. You know that Panos is taking advantage of the situation to test your attitude towards Matt. Do you:

Play him along and make your response deliberately evasive?	Turn to 57
Say bluntly that you have no interest in Matt Jardine since you already have a boyfriend back in England?	Turn to 119

132

The book seems to have been written by a British resident and published privately. It's fairly heavy reading, though sprinkled with the occasional anecdote reflecting the islanders' idiosyncratic outlook on life. Flicking through, your eye is caught by the name of Simnaki, the little nearby island. It comes in the tale of Yanni Lamoulis, an old drunkard who was driven out of his house by his wife one night because he staggered home drunk. Bemoaning his fate to the stars, he sought shelter from a freak summer storm in the old ruined temple of Aphrodite – too drunk to care about the old tale of ghosts there. And that was the last anyone heard of him for a week or more. It was assumed that he had fallen off a cliff that night and his body had been washed away in the stormy seas. Then the poor man was found wandering through an olive grove right over the other side of the island, babbling of spirits and gold. He can't have eaten for days, his body was sadly emaciated and his mind was clearly gone. All he could say was that the fairies had taken him to see Aphrodite, seated on a golden throne, and the goddess had bid him stay. 'I want to go back! Please let me go back!' he would cry piteously.

After many months of care and treatment old Yanni's memory returned and he began to behave more normally. But he wouldn't touch a drop of alcohol and spent much of his time wandering around the old temple. Then, one day, he disappeared again, this time for good. His wife and friends mourned his death and threw flowers into the harbour at his funeral, though his body was never found.

The legend says that old Yanni finally met the goddess again and went to serve her in her palace of gold.

You close the book and switch off the light and wonder sleepily what on earth could have happened to the old man in the week he was lost. Where could he have been? Could the ruined temple hold some ancient secret?

Turn to 32

133

Penny's always game for a bit of adventure. You worm your way into the crowd seated around the fire, and manage to get next to her. You suggest a trip over to Simnaki for a picnic tomorrow.

'That's a brilliant idea,' she squeals, 'but how do we get there?'

'I can take you over to the island,' interrupts the boy sitting behind you. You recognize him as Lars, one of Liam's fellow diggers.

'I am going over later than the others as I have a few things to do in town first. I'll be rowing over about eleven o'clock. You're very welcome to hitch a ride, but you'll have to make your own way back unless you want to hang round until sundown.'

What a piece of luck. Excitedly, you and Penny begin to plan your day.

Turn to 341

134

Boris's leer broadens as he recognizes you, and your heart sinks as you remember your last encounter.

'Well, now. It's my little runaway. Changed your mind about me have you, then? Couldn't wait to get a little more action, huh? Come closer, honey, and see what I've got for you!' His voice thickens as he moves to kiss you. How do you react?

Try to knee him	Turn to **82**
Scream and struggle	Turn to **40**

135

This news hits you like a bombshell. July 14th. That's the day after tomorrow! Something tells you that for Nigel to come out to Simnos now would be disastrous for both of you. On the other hand if he has his heart set on this holiday who are you to put the dampers on it? You mull this problem over in your mind until you fall asleep in the early hours of the morning. When you wake up the next day, you have still not reached a conclusion as to what course of action you should take. Perhaps you should ask someone's advice. Who will you turn to?

Penny	Turn to **289**
Panos	Turn to **245**
Matt	Turn to **193**
None of these	Turn to **301**

136

Unfortunately, the combination of the wind and the tide are too much for you. You struggle on bravely for several more minutes but it soon becomes clear that you are making no headway. Sick with frustration and disappointment you turn the board round and head back inland, resolving to try again some other time.

Lose 1 Luck point.

Turn to **254**

137

Panos deposits you at the local taverna whilst he delivers the spares to his uncle's farm. His excuse for not inviting you along too is that if you were both to appear, his aunt would insist upon you staying for lunch, and that would take up too much of the day. You, however, have a strong suspicion that Panos's reluctance to introduce you to his family might have something to do with this mysterious Greek girlfriend he pretends doesn't exist. Still, who are you to kick up a fuss about it? You have a boyfriend back home, and Panos *is* just a friend – at the moment.

You have consumed two lemonades, a Greek coffee and a slice of *baklava* when Panos finally returns looking rather harassed.

'Greek hospitality,' he explains. 'You call in for a minute and they try to turn the occasion into a party!' He smiles in such a winning way it's hard to be cross for long.

'Right, where to now?' you ask, ready for action.

'How about the ancient monastery of Aghios Dionysus?' suggests Panos. 'There are lots of interesting things to see, and the view is quite spectacular.'

'Sounds fine to me,' you reply enthusiastically.

Panos insists on settling the bill and very soon you are roaring off into the distance at full throttle.

Turn to **243**

138

You are bound hand and foot and left in the outer chamber of the *tholos*, while they continue to carry the treasure down to the beach. You notice that there is only the space of two or three minutes each time, in which you are not under observation. This could be a slim chance to escape.

Are the Fates with you? Throw a die.

1–3   Turn to **34**

4–6   Turn to **164**

139

'The heat plays strange tricks with the mind, you know,' suggests Panos in disbelief.

You are adamant that he is not going to make you back down and say you imagined the incident. Furiously, you set about finishing the repairs on the scooter.

'OK, so what did he look like then, this . . . this villain?' You cannot help smiling at Panos's choice of vocabulary.

'A fat, greasy slob . . . balding . . . late thirties, early forties . . . nasty expression . . . oh, and some sort of tattoo on his arm. Looked like a snake from where I was.'

Panos stiffens at this last piece of information. It's as if he knows something, but he's not going to let on. 'Sounds like a nasty piece of work,' he says. 'Let's hope he didn't get a good look at you.'

Turn to 53

140

You struggle but to very little effect. The man is immensely strong. You fill your lungs and are about to give vent to an ear-shattering scream, when your attacker's attention is apparently caught by something behind him. You seize the opportunity to knee him in a painful place and, as he doubles up in agony, clench your fists together and bring them down hard on the back of his neck. He slumps to the ground cursing, but is clearly made of resilient stuff as he almost immediately starts getting to his feet again. You sensibly decide not to hang around and run off, making several twists and turns down little alleyways in an effort to shake off a pursuit. This seems to work. Nobody is following you. When you have recovered yourself a bit, you make your way back down to the waterfront and then home to the villa, pondering on this nasty attack. What could have distracted your assailant? There didn't seem to be anyone there when you freed yourself, though you might have caught sight of a movement in a doorway as you ran off. Very strange.

Turn to 324

141

Looking back over your time on Simnos you feel a sense of satisfaction at having taken the opportunity to spread your wings and learn about life in a foreign country. You might feel that you have also learnt a fair bit about yourself, but it is probable that you are still having difficulty in deciding where your romantic preference lies. It is so difficult to know who to believe and who to trust . . . Now you have got used to your work at the villa, the cooking, cleaning and shopping take only a fraction of the time it used to, and you find yourself with much more free time. The afternoons are generally spent on the beach, swimming and sunbathing. You have even had a go at scuba diving and water skiing, but your favourite water sport is still windsurfing, which you seem to have taken to with remarkable ease. A new batch of guests has arrived, and you and Penny are both relieved to see the back of the fractious Donna at last, but a little sad to say good-bye to Greg who had become a friend. You are half-way through the summer, but you are already considering what possibilities are open to you on your return. One thing is for sure, now you have broadened your horizons by working abroad, you know you must move away from home – possibly to London to find a job in the travel business. Or perhaps you might try and work in a ski-resort in France or Austria during the winter months.

But first there's this job to finish. Could there be any problems with that? Over the last few weeks fragments of information you have gleaned, rumours you have heard, incidents you have wit-nessed, all might suggest that there is something not quite right on the island. Could it possibly involve you?

Before you embark upon the next stage of your adventure, there is a question that must be answered: recently you received two letters from Nigel. Did you read both of them?

If you read the first letter
   only   Turn to **175**
If you read both letters   Turn to **333**

142

The track continues to rise and the olive groves gradually give way to shrub. A gentle breeze from the sea refreshes you, though you realize that on a stormy day, incredibly high winds must buffet this hill.

'There it is!' shouts Liam. 'That's Castro.'

At first you see nothing, then you realize that the odd-shaped humps ahead of you are moss-covered stones. You both park your mopeds under a tree and head into the old fort.

Turn to 344

143

Matt is pontificating about literature to an intense-looking young man with a straggly beard.

You wait until there is a suitable gap in the conversation and Matt's audience has gone off to refill his glass, then swiftly sit yourself down next to him.

'What are you doing tomorrow, Matt?' you inquire tentatively.

Matt looks intrigued. 'Why, have you something interesting in mind?'

'How does a trip over to Simnaki grab you? We could take a picnic and make a day of it. I've been on Simnos weeks now, and I still haven't had a look at the dig.'

'Oh, you haven't missed much. Besides, the archaeologists aren't too keen on strangers poking about. It's serious work, you know . . .'

'But the island doesn't belong to the archaeologists. We've got as much right to be there as they have. Besides, I'm genuinely interested in ancient history. Anyway, you can talk. I've heard you're always sneaking off there, and you've never once offered to take me along.'

'I only go over to the island when I feel the need to be completely alone – I go in search of inspiration . . .' replies Matt, a hint of exasperation creeping into his voice.

'What's the big mystery about the island? You act as if there's something out there you don't want me to see?' you venture provocatively.

Matt laughs loudly. 'OK, OK, you win,' he relents, giving you a friendly hug. 'I'll take you across tomorrow. My rowing boat has sprung a few leaks I'm afraid – I hope you're a good swimmer!'

Turn to **231**

It is a long, terrifying drop and, as you plunge into the sea, your arm strikes a hidden rock which gives you a nasty graze. You are in no fit state to swim.

Lose 1 Luck point.

You drag yourself back to the beach, where you find a reception committee of Burke and Matt Jardine waiting for you. There is no escape and you are bundled roughly aboard their launch, which is now moored at the far end of the beach, bound hand and foot and locked into the cabin.

Turn to **260**

145

'Thanks a bunch. I've just spent twenty minutes covering myself in oil, and you swan past and kick a whole sand dune over me.' You hope you sound suitably indignant.

'Please excuse my carelessness. But perhaps you are over-reacting a little, yes?'

Totally unprepared for such a remark you open and close your mouth dumbly.

'I mean,' he continues, 'if you come down to the beach, you are expecting to come into contact with a little bit of sand.' He smiles amiably. 'There are freshwater showers at the beach taverna. Come, you can get rid of this horrible sand and I will buy you a drink to make amends. OK?

Do you:

Relent and accept Panos's invitation?	Turn to **37**
Refuse his invitation?	Turn to **151**

You find Liam immersed in a highly detailed conversation with one of the other students on the dig. With some difficulty, you attract his attention and draw him to one side, out of earshot, and tell him everything you have discovered.

'I knew it!' he exclaims. 'There's been something fishy about this dig right from the beginning! So that's it!'

'Shouldn't we go to the police with this evidence?' you ask.

'Well,' he pauses, thinking hard. 'We could – but I don't think that would get us very far. You see, even if they believed us, it would be dead easy for Burke and the rest to make up a plausible story to account for the treasure's presence in the tomb. And we haven't got much time.'

'So what do we do? Try to catch them in the act?'

Liam's face lights up with excitement.

'Yes, that's it! We'll catch them in the act! Tonight!'

You quickly make a plan to meet and then leave the island. You have a hectic evening at the villa and have little time to think about the day's events until you retire to bed. It takes you a long time to get to sleep.

Turn to **346**

Today is market day in Simnos town, and the labyrinthine streets have the atmosphere of the bazaar about them. You jostle your way through, edging warily around the hind-quarters of sleepy-eyed donkeys laden with huge paniers full of produce . . . succulent red tomatoes, watermelons the size of footballs, lemons, cucumbers . . . a riot of colour contrasting with the icy white of the buildings. The Post Office is bustling as usual, mostly due to the hordes of tourists buying stamps for holiday postcards. On one side of the counter is a large cardboard box divided into alphabetical sections with POSTE RESTANTE scrawled across it in wobbly biro. You sort through the dog-eared envelopes with foreign postmarks and pick out two letters in Nigel's handwriting. You examine the postmarks. Although the letters were posted several days apart, the erratic nature of the postal system to Simnos has caused them to be delivered together. You keep the first letter and stuff the second into your bag to read later.

Perhaps there is something interesting awaiting Penny. You flip through the Vs – Van der Guyt . . . Varenne . . . Vitulli . . .

Does the name Vitulli mean anything to you?

Yes	Turn to **19**
No	Turn to **65**

148

With a cry of triumph, Liam spots that there is an air-lock in the moped's fuel line. Within a few, rather messy minutes, the thing is fixed and the pair of you set off again.

Turn to 142

149

Aphrodite, Goddess of Love, appears to be feeling a degree of hostility towards you at this time. Lose 3 Luck points.

Nigel's visit to Simnos has caused you much embarrassment, not to mention guilt over the past week. His clinging presence has dominated your free time, and distracted you from your work at the villa, so that a few of the guests have begun to grumble about your lack of concern. The way things are going, you will not only soon be losing your friends, but also your job. You decide the time has come to talk things out. You explain firmly that you need a breathing space to reconsider your relationship, and suggest a trial separation. Nigel returns to England at the end of the week in very gloomy spirits, leaving you with a battered conscience.

Now it's up to you to pick up the threads of your adventure. You have had your ups and downs but who knows what the future will bring? Excitement, drama, romance . . .

Turn to 141

150

The cool air outside the disco is very refreshing. You walk to the farthest edge of the isthmus and look out to sea, marvelling at the clearness of the night sky, sparkled with more stars than you ever see at home. Liam takes a great delight in pointing out landmarks to you, including the massive luxury yacht anchored in the bay, which he says belongs to the shipping millionaire, Georgios Koutalas.

Liam has a summer job working on the archaeological dig on the little island of Simnaki but seems a bit reluctant to tell you much about it.

Will you press him to tell you
more?   Turn to 302

Or would you rather return to
the disco?   Turn to 178

151

Panos shakes his head sorrowfully. 'Ah, you English girls are so proud,' he complains, trying to look crestfallen.

Perhaps you have been a bit harsh.

'Not proud, just busy,' you reply cheerfully. 'I've got to get to the shops before they close for the *siesta* or I won't have anything to cook for dinner tonight.'

You explain about your job and Penny's hangover.

Then you remember you have something to ask Panos.

Turn to 5

152

Realizing that it is probably best not to take this further, you make some non-committal reply and turn the conversation to other topics. Matt shoots a suspicious look at you but does not press you further.

Are the Fates with you? Throw a die.

1–3	Turn to **228**
4–6	Turn to **300**

153

You grab a barbecued chicken leg and a plastic beaker full of antiseptic-smelling wine and go to sit on a ridge of rocks by the water's edge. You watch from a distance, feeling removed from the gaiety of the scene. A gentle splash splash on the water turns your attention seawards. The shadow of a small rubber dinghy is heading silently for the adjacent cove. Intrigued, you scramble along the rocks to get a better look. The mystery rower drags the dinghy up the beach and into one of the caves carved into the cliff. As he moves away from the shadow of the cliffs on to the moonlit expanse of the beach you recognize the silhouetted form of Garth.

You jump down on to the sand expecting to surprise him, but Garth refuses to be ruffled.

'Funny time of night to be out for a row, isn't it?' you inquire, with a measure of impertinence.

'Why not?' Garth replies easily. 'It's therapeutic. Puts one's thoughts in order.'

Do you:

Suggest Garth puts his dinghy
  to good use and takes you to
  the island tomorrow?   Turn to **247**
Say nothing and resolve to
  keep an eye on his activities?   Turn to **133**

154

Are the Fates with you? Throw a die.

1–3   Turn to **240**
4–6   Turn to **342**

155

A noisy group are drinking cocktails by the pool-side. You select a sunlounger in the shade and lie back to observe them from a discreet distance. After some minutes a young man dressed in threadbare khaki shorts and a crumpled shirt joins you. This is Liam MacNamara, a young archaeology student who is working on the excavations at Simnaki. Liam is always ready to chat on his subject, but you find him rather too serious for your liking. Stuck in the groove of the past, he often seems like a fish out of water in the present.

'Mind if I join you?'

'Not at all,' you nod at the adjacent lounger.

For want of a better topic of conversation you ask him how the dig is going.

'Not very well I'm afraid,' he begins.

'Oh oh, here we go,' you say to yourself.

'The main problem is our project leader. Dr McHenry, the archaeologist who planned the excavation, had to retire owing to ill health, and so Koutalas, who is funding the dig, brought in this American, Orlando Burke. Quite frankly, I don't think he knows a sarcophagus from an amphora.'

For the first time even-tempered Liam appears quite overwrought. 'It's almost as if we are jinxed,' he continues. 'A while ago all the diagrams of the Sanctuary went missing from the monastery of Aghios Dionysus. Our findings so far have been very disappointing, although according to my calculations the temple of Aphrodite should have been the repository of huge riches. . . .'

He tails off in mid-sentence as a middle-aged man in a white safari suit, his neck swathed in gold chains, teeters towards you clutching a large tumbler full of what looks like neat whisky.

'Everything to your liking, Liam? Beats sweltering in the heat all day amongst the ruins, eh?'

'Yes, Dr Burke. It's great,' answers Liam in a flat voice.

Burke raises his glass in a toast. 'Here's to Aphrodite, Goddess of Love and Fertility,' he slurs, and stumbles off towards the pool.

'Bit of a drink problem,' explains Liam.

But you are not listening. Where have you heard that voice before? A snatch of overheard conversation comes back to you: 'It's not like digging up potatoes, you know . . .' You deliberate about sharing this discovery with Liam. But share what? A half-heard snatch of conversation? Nothing incriminating was said, after all. You let Liam rabbit on about his passion for archaeology, whilst trying to piece together in your own mind the various fragments of what you have seen and heard this afternoon.

Turn to **43**

156

Are the Fates with you? Throw a die.

1–3	Turn to **272**
4–6	Turn to **284**

157

Mustering a relaxed smile you shrug nonchalantly.

'I work with Penny at To Limani. She's been telling me so much about you. I thought I would call by and introduce myself while I was up this way. I didn't mean to cause any offence.'

Matt looks slightly embarrassed at his outburst and makes an effort to recover his composure.

'Well, I suppose it could be argued that I should have locks put on the door if I actively want to discourage visitors. Look, I'm sorry I lost my cool just now. Here, sit down and I'll open some beer – warm, I'm afraid, there's no fridge.'

He opens two bottles of lager and clears a space for them on the table.

'Sorry about the mess . . . People in my profession are notoriously untidy.'

'You're a writer, aren't you?'

'Supposedly.'

'Penny says you're *supposed* to be vaguely famous.'

Matt does his best to appear unaffected by this remark, but you detect a glimmer of conceit in his eyes.

'Appeals to your romantic nature, does it . . . penetrating the "inner sanctum" of a "vaguely famous" writer?' he asks, waving a negligent hand at the chaos around him.

Before you have time to come back with a suitably crushing remark, a loud rapping at the shutters makes you both start.

Turn to **283**

158

Your heart thumps as he starts to speak. He tells you how much he likes you – and also that he's a bit of a loner. He also says that he has a vacancy at his agency, for a smart young trainee and he offers the job to you. You'd be based in London, have a good salary – and plenty of opportunity to see Garth. The only snag is that he was on the point of offering it to someone else, so if you want the job, you'll have to take it immediately. This would mean leaving for London tomorrow. What do you say? Will you take the job?

Yes   Turn to **222**
No   Turn to **56**

Matt unties you and you fall into his arms with relief. Matt's theory about this whole operation is that it is not technically theft, since if Koutalas and his gang had not located the treasure, it could have remained undetected, probably forever. In your heart of hearts, you know that Matt is a flawed character, but there is a strong magnetic quality about him that you find you cannot resist, and you see in him the chance to escape from the mundane life that awaits you back home. Now he is sure of your allegiance, Matt confides that they are planning to shift the treasure that night. A small yacht will be waiting at 3.30 am to take the four of you and the priceless cargo to Piraeus, the port of Athens. From there, the treasure will be loaded by Koutalas's men into a merchant vessel bound for Panama. Once it has arrived at its destination, it will be distributed through an underground network into the collections of private individuals who will pay handsomely in Swiss francs with no questions asked for such exquisite and rare items. You and Matt will catch a morning flight from Athens to Amsterdam, having collected *en route* an envelope containing one million US dollars in used notes, deposited in a left-luggage locker at the airport. From Amsterdam you will fly to Lima, Peru. Fortunately, you have acquired the habit of carrying your passport with you at all times, and therefore you have no need to return to the villa.

Turn to 281

160

You are lucky. The noise of the fall appears to have gone unnoticed. After a terrifying moment as you wait for a shout of discovery, you pull yourself up and look in at the window again. At the far end of the hut, you can see a dark figure hunched over a small camping gas stove, methodically burning papers and collecting the ash in a tin bowl. As he turns to reach for a new batch of papers you see that the figure is none other than Orlando Burke! And the papers must be something very incriminating! They could be the proof that you are after. What will you do?

Try some ruse to get hold of
the papers   Turn to **200**
Leave it and head down to the
tholos   Turn to **116**

You arrive on the jetty ten minutes before midday. Luckily, Matt is already waiting in the launch and you set off immediately, avoiding a possible encounter with Panos.

The sight of the immaculate white hull of the boat *Hera* sends a tremor of apprehension through you. What sort of people will you find aboard the yacht? Will they all be glamorous, successful and rich? What will they think of you in your simple cotton dress that seems to be growing shabbier by the minute?

'Tell me again how you know Koutalas,' you ask Matt, wanting to get a few details straight in your mind before you disembark. Matt leans back and draws meditatively on his cigarette.

'Oh, I met him in New York several times. My agent introduced us a few years ago, just after I had completed *The Mazeppa Circle*. I bumped into him again last summer in a club in Vegas.'

'What sort of club?'

'Well, a casino actually. Not that I'm into gambling myself,' he adds, seeing your look of disapproval. 'Koutalas is crazy for it though – roulette, poker, blackjack, you name it. They say half his empire is built with cash from lucky wins.'

The engine of the launch cuts out and you glide up to the boarding ladder. Up on deck you glimpse flashes of colour, blond heads, brown skin. The sound of laughter and the chinking of glasses drifts down to you below.

Turn to **313**

Hearing their names works like magic on Garth's dogs. They return to the veranda and lie there, huge pink tongues lolling out of their mouths. Rather gingerly, you knock at the front door and getting no answer, push it open.

The villa appears to be deserted, but you get the feeling that Garth cannot have gone far. He had obviously begun preparing a salad lunch for himself before he left. Penny looks round the rest of the villa, while you poke about in the living room. Several papers lie scattered on the table and one in particular catches your eye. It is a list of names, with notes scrawled by them. You are surprised to see Matt Jardine's name linked to Georgios Koutalas and a question mark is by Liam MacNamara. Before you have time to study the sheet further, a step sounds outside and you hurriedly place it back on the table. Garth comes into the room and does a double-take when he sees you there. Penny emerges behind him and accuses him of having forgotten all about the party on the yacht.

'Is it that time already? Sorry, girls, I guess I clean forgot the time. Just let me wash and brush up and I'll be with you.'

The *Hera* is a luxury-class yacht, massive, immaculate, looking more like a mansion than a boat inside. Your host fits perfectly into his surroundings. Short, stubby figure, going slightly to fat, Koutalas wears a white silk suit and several gold rings. He greets his guests with a broad smile, which somehow never seems to reach his eyes.

'Garth, dear boy, how delightful that you could come.' He takes your hand. 'And how kind of you to bring two such charming young ladies!'

Penny and you exchange glances.

'Let me tear you away from them for a moment, there's someone I particularly want you to meet.'

So speaking, he bears Garth off inexorably.

'Charming,' explodes Penny.

Just then she spots Matt Jardine and suggests that you join him. What will you do?

Go with Penny to see Matt   Turn to **250**
Wander around on your own   Turn to **112**

163

Liam leads you down a dark stone corridor into a vaulted chamber with a high domed ceiling. The warm fetid air makes you feel claustrophobic, but your curiosity will not allow you to turn back.

'You can always determine the wealth of ancient civilizations by their burial customs,' he announces, waving his flashlight around the circular chamber, as if he were showing you the guestroom of a new house. This macabre talk makes you shiver in spite of the warmth.

'Don't worry,' he says in a practical voice, 'we've removed all the skeletons . . . Look at the magnificent high domed ceiling. These tombs are often called "beehive" tombs because of their shape.'

You make a few appreciative noises and suggest

that perhaps you should return to the daylight. But your guide has more treats up his sleeve.

'What is so special about these tombs is that they each have a hidden inner chamber which must have been utilized for the safe storage of treasure. Look here.' He crawls through what looks like a hole in the wall and bids you follow. Gingerly you obey. You straighten up to find yourself in a small room, decorated with the crumbling remains of frescoes. Liam draws your attention to a higher corner stone inscribed with a distinctive sign that you have noticed on many occasions during your stay on Simnos. He explains that this is the sign of the goddess Aphrodite, marking the secret hiding-place where the wealth of the dead was secreted.

'Let's pull out the stone and have a look. You try, it should come away quite easily,' he coaxes. You have a feeling that you might be about to discover something exciting. You give the stone a good tug but it is wedged firm.

Are the Fates with you? Flip a coin.

Heads	Turn to 75
Tails	Turn to 11

164

However much you struggle with the tapes that bind you, you cannot break them. Eventually, the villains finish loading the treasure, bundle you roughly down to the beach and lock you into the cabin of their launch.

Turn to **260**

Panos's Greek pride might have suffered a slight battering but he is not going to give up so easily.

'OK – perhaps I see you at the Black Cat tonight?'

You make a tentative promise to meet, loath to commit yourself to a firm arrangement. Who knows what might turn up! Panos's attention is distracted by the sight of Matt shambling out of the Post Office. He appears to be heading in your direction. Panos does not wait to acknowledge Matt's arrival on the scene, but rides off down the street at a furious pace, leaving a cloud of yellow dust in his wake.

Matt's trip to the Post Office must have been a fruitful one; two thick airmail letters protrude from his breast pocket.

'Hi,' he says confidently. 'I thought you might be in need of rescuing.'

What do you say?

'Thanks – things were getting
   rather heavy.'   Turn to **179**
'Panos happens to be a friend of
   mine, and I don't need rescuing
   from him.'   Turn to **23**

166

Garth Craigmillar looks extremely disappointed and Donna is clearly furious. She says some fairly unpleasant things before ushering her guest out, promising to write to Villalink about the unhelpfulness of their staff. Lose 1 Luck point. You decide not to risk a further tongue-lashing and nip off to bed.

Turn to 320

167

Unthinkingly, you blurt out that this is extremely odd, because there appeared to be no letters addressed in his name when you went through the box five minutes ago. Matt looks frankly displeased, and too late you realize your indiscretion.

'Regular little sleuth, aren't you?' he comments with sarcasm. 'Perhaps you didn't search the box as thoroughly as you imagined . . .'

The revving of a scooter interrupts this uncomfortable dialogue. Panos, clad not in his customary red swimming trunks, but a pair of stone-washed jeans and a 'Frankie Goes to Hollywood' T-shirt, coasts up alongside you. The two men acknowledge each other with a formal nod.

'I'm sure you two kids have a whole lot to talk about,' says Matt, obviously anxious to take his leave. 'See you around.'

He saunters off, leaving you still puzzled at his behaviour. Were you mistaken about the letter? Why should Matt choose to lie about it.

Turn to 131

It's all over in moments. With a sickening thud, Liam crashes to the ground and lies still. From this distance, you have no way of telling whether he is still alive, or not. His assailant then swiftly completes the destruction of the precious map, before slapping his companion conscious again. After a brief, heated argument, which seems to concern Liam, they leave him where he is and climb back up the tunnel. Once you are sure they have gone, you scutter over to Liam's body, your heart thudding with panic. To your relief, he is still alive, though clearly badly hurt. Gradually he regains consciousness and, with much groaning, hauls himself to his feet. His first thought is of the map and, when he registers its total destruction, his gloom deepens.

'Where were you when I needed you?' he asks accusingly.

You have nothing to say. Lose 1 Luck point for your cowardice.

Slowly you make your way back up the tunnel. You rest for a while at the top, out in the fresh air.

'What do we do now?' You turn to Liam anxiously. He looks worried.

'Don't say a word about this to anybody,' he replies in a low, urgent voice. 'Those were no ordinary vandals. I reckon we've stumbled on something big!'

'But shouldn't we tell the police?'

'What for? The map's beyond rescue now. They wouldn't do anything – and we've no proof.'

You decide to head for home. How did you come to Castro?

By donkey   Turn to 74
By moped   Turn to 42

169

Matt tilts your chin in his hand and kisses you on the mouth. After a short time, you break away, indicating your embarrassment in the presence of the driver. Matt waves aside your protest with a laugh.

'Don't be so prudish,' he says, 'he's Greek. Greece is the land of romance.'

Walking home hand in hand up the cliff path to To Limani, your thoughts turn momentarily to Nigel, an image you push well to the back of your mind. You suggest meeting later at the Black Cat, but Matt says he has reached a difficult passage in his book and wants to concentrate on it this evening.

'Still, there's plenty of time for us to get better acquainted,' he says, leaving you with a long, lingering kiss. You watch him make his way up the track to the windmill.

Turn to 47

Penny looks frankly astonished when you say that you had planned to go to the old fort, and not much pleased. In her unpredictable fashion, she seems to have decided that you are just being perverse and tries to persuade you to change your mind. And when you explain that the expedition will take the whole day, she becomes rather cross.

'Why should I cover for you?' she asks pettishly.

You hold back your instinctive reaction that you cover for her often enough when she's got a hangover, realizing that provoking an argument is hardly likely to get you anywhere. You're annoyed to see that Garth seems highly amused by the exchange, while Liam visibly wishes he could be elsewhere. It is perhaps this evidence of his craven attitude that strengthens your resolve and you ask Penny again whether she will cover for you.

Are the Fates with you? Throw a dice.

1–3   Turn to **184**
4–6   Turn to **50**

171

'Still. After tonight it'll be all over. I'll have plenty of cash to start a new life. I guess I'll lie low in South America for a few years. Then perhaps I'll resurface as a writer when all this has blown over . . . when all that remains of the scandal of Simnaki is just a vague memory and a few faded newspaper cuttings.'

'Aren't you forgetting something?' you ask quietly. 'What about me?'

From Matt's expression you can tell that this is one part of his scheme that has not yet been given due consideration. His forehead furrows into a frown. For a few seconds you stare at each other as if in suspended animation. Then, he leans over and softly strokes your anxious face. With a stifled sob he buries his face in your hair and murmurs almost inaudibly: 'Come with me.'

What will you answer be?

Yes   Turn to **159**
No   Turn to **215**

172

Feeling very sorry for yourself and aware that you are going to be as stiff as a board tomorrow, you leave Liam to sort out paying Angelis and take your aching bones back to the villa.

Turn to **47**

173

Aphrodite, Goddess of Love, has smiled upon you. Gain 2 Luck points.

On Nigel's last evening on Simnos, after a heated discussion about whether you should hand in your notice or remain on the island, he stomps off alone to the Black Cat. Fortunately for you, this night he falls in with a group of German students who are planning to spend the next week island hopping, and they invite him to join them (you suspect that he has more than a passing interest in one of the girls in the party). The next day Nigel leaves Simnos with his new friends and your parting is amicable. Who can tell what will happen when you return to England in the autumn, but for now the important thing is that you are free to pick up your adventure again.

Turn to 141

174

About half an hour later, you are interrupted by a knock on the front door of the villa and quickly go to see who could be calling at this time of night.

Opening the door reveals a tall, athletically built man, possibly in his late twenties, with pleasant, if not handsome features. Judging by his carefully creased but fashionable trousers and loose shirt, he is a man who cares about his appearance but not obsessively. Russet hair above warm brown eyes and a smile that immediately prompts a return smile from you.

'Hello, I'm Garth Craigmillar.'

'. . . from the other villa," you interrupt, and then laugh.

Your visitor laughs, too.

'I only came to ask . . .'

Just then, you are disturbed by Donna Chadwick, who clearly wants to poke her nose in. She invites Garth Craigmillar in for some coffee and then rather pointedly orders you off to the kitchen to prepare it.

'No, thank you,' says Garth in his soft voice, 'though it's kind of you to offer. I really only came to ask whether I could use your telephone. It's too late to get down to town and something has cropped up in the States.' He looks at you inquiringly.

Before you have a chance to answer, Donna gushes, 'Oh, of course you can. Anything we can do to help.' Garth Craigmillar seems to have made an instant impression on her and you can only feel glad that her husband, Steve, isn't in the hall to witness her performance.

The telephone is in the annexe, just outside Penny's room, and is not normally available for the use of guests unless there is an emergency. All calls have to be recorded in the phone book and paid for. This is a dilemma. Donna had absolutely no right to offer the phone to a visitor, but in refusing his request you are bound to appear churlish. It would help to put Donna in her place, but might alienate this rather attractive stranger.

What do you do?

Offer to show him the phone	Turn to 114
Say he can't use it	Turn to 166

Lose 2 Luck points.

Had you taken the trouble to read Nigel's second letter, you would have learnt that he was planning to come out to Simnos on a surprise visit. You are sitting peacefully in a café on the harbour with one of your male friends (this could be Matt, Garth, Liam or Panos, depending upon who you have been spending more time with recently), when you notice a familiar-looking boy stepping off the ferry. Imagine your shock when you realize that it is Nigel! Nigel is delighted to see you, he assumes that you have read his letter and have come to meet him. The truth of the matter, that his visit is a complete surprise to you, and not a very pleasant one at that, makes him furious. He accuses you of two-timing, and there is a nasty scene between you up at the villa, within earshot of several guests. You warn Nigel to keep away from the villa in future, but he refuses, and you sense that you have lost popularity with the guests. Eventually, a couple of them actually complain to the Villalink offices that you are not doing your job properly, and you receive a stiff phone call from the Managing Director of the company recalling you to London.

Back home, enduring the dull routine of work in an insurance company, you are reading the paper one lunchtime when an interesting headline catches your eye:

GREEK ISLAND TREASURE SCANDAL

A short report follows telling how a gang of international art racketeers were arrested smuggling a priceless collection of antiquities from the holiday-makers' paradise island of Simnos. The identity of the smugglers is not revealed. You *thought* there was something fishy going on. Perhaps if you had stayed on the island you could have done something to prevent this happening . . . Who knows?

Your adventure ends here.

Check your score at the back of the book, then go back to 1 and see if you reach a more satisfactory and exciting conclusion next time.

176

You manage to grab his arm and prevent him leaping forward to prevent the destruction of the map. Silent and horrified, you watch as the two vandals complete their task, shuddering as the sound of the pick rings round the small chamber and huge chips of stone fly off the wall. Eventually, they seem satisfied by their handiwork and make their way back up the tunnel. When you are sure that they have gone, you creep out of your hiding-place.

Liam's little torch shows only too well how complete the destruction has been. No sign of the map remains at all.

Gloomily, you make your way back up the tunnel.

'What do we do now?' You turn to Liam anxiously. He looks worried.

'Don't say a word about this to anybody,' he replies in a low urgent voice. 'Those were no ordinary vandals. I reckon we've stumbled on something big.'

'But shouldn't we tell the police?'

'What for? The map's beyond rescue now. They wouldn't do anything – and we've no proof.'

You decide to head for home. How did you get here?

| By donkey | Turn to 74 |
| By moped | Turn to 42 |

177

Matt guides you skilfully up the path. It is now quite dark, but he is so familiar with the lie of the land that a flashlight would be superfluous.

'Hmm. Quite athletic for a woman,' he drawls teasingly as the gradient increases.

'I need to be fit,' you reply sweetly. 'I have to work for a living.'

'Come on, don't tell me you're out here to work,

honey. You're here to have a good time like the rest of them. Discos, watersports, lazing on the beach . . .'

'I'm not interested in lazing all day on beaches,' you retaliate with annoyance.

'Don't like the beach, eh? Wait until you've met the guy who runs the windsurfing school, Panos his name is. You'll soon change your mind about the beach once you've run into him a couple of times.'

You are about to protest when Matt stops dead in his tracks and grabs you by the arm. Lurking by the windmill is the silhouette of a man – obviously awaiting Matt's return.

'Er, listen, honey,' says Matt, 'I forgot, an old business friend of mine said he might call in tonight. We've got one or two things to discuss before he goes back to the States. Perhaps we could postpone our date?'

Infuriated at having made the long climb for nothing, you stomp back down to the villa, vowing that one day you will teach Matt Jardine a lesson.

Turn to 320

178

'I think I'll stay here a bit,' Liam says. 'I've got a few things to work out.'

He doesn't say any more and clearly would rather be on his own, so you leave him there.

Turn to 98

179

Matt is delighted to have the opportunity to get one over on Panos, whom he plainly resents for his easy charm and natural good looks. He is well aware that he cannot compete with Panos in a contest of beauty, but he knows that he would come out top any day in a contest of intellect. Matt's arrogance has often caused your temper to rise, but you cannot help feeling drawn to him. Without talking, you stroll towards the harbour together. The waterfront of Simnos town has been dominated for the last few weeks by the huge white hull of the *Hera*, a massive luxury yacht belonging to Georgios Koutalas, a Greek shipping magnate of international notoriety. You comment upon the beauty of the vessel.

'Would you like to see inside?' asks Matt casually.

'Of course, who wouldn't?'

'You could come aboard with me if you like. I've run into Koutalas a couple of times here and there,' he continues, revelling in your incredulity. 'He's holding a reception tomorrow lunchtime, and I've received a formal invitation. Meet me tomorrow at the jetty at twelve. There will be a motor launch to take us out to the yacht.'

'I'll be there!' you shout back excitedly, as you tear off to confide your stroke of good fortune to Penny. Sprinting up the path, something odd occurs to you. When Matt emerged from the Post Office he was carrying two airmail letters, yet when you examined the contents of the Poste Restante box five minutes before there were certainly no letters addressed in his name . . .

Turn to **35**

180

Unfortunately, Burke is made of sterner stuff than you had thought. Just as you reach the end of your shriek, a heavy hand falls on your shoulder and spins you around. It is Orlando Burke! He must have crept out of the hut without you noticing and made his way round behind you to catch you in the act. The hand that holds the gun is as steady as a rock and you are his prisoner.

Lose 1 Luck point.

Turn to **138**

181

Down on the beach it looks like recriminations are flying between Panos and the dark-haired girl. Looking back on the scene from the sanctuary of the beach bar you feel relieved that you made your getaway before this little domestic dispute got going. After a few minutes Panos has had enough, and shrugging off the girl's protests with a gesture of impatience, he stomps off huffily to resume his work. Shame. You were just getting on so well together. Wondering whether Panos will remember his invitation of a trip to the small island, you try and fix your mind on your shopping list and head for the town.

Turn to **63**

182

Liam rolls the boulder back into place and makes a careful note of its position so that he'll know where to find it when he returns. You wander round the old town a bit more but find nothing else of interest. Eventually, you decide that time is getting on and that you should go home. How did you come to Castro?

By donkey   Turn to **74**
By moped   Turn to **42**

183

You point out to Matt that lots of people have hard lives, but it doesn't have to turn you into a criminal. Your captor is not in the mood for criticism.

'I thought you of all people would understand,' he reproaches.

'It's not too late, you know. You could come to the police with me now. I take it you've found the treasure?'

Matt jumps to his feet trembling.

'No, no, no,' he shouts. 'I'm not going back now. You can't make me.' His tone reminds you of a spoilt child trying to get his own way. 'If I can't trust you to keep your mouth shut about whatever you might have seen, we'll have to think of a way to make sure you don't blab to anyone.'

He unties the rope around your legs and drags you to your feet.

'Move it,' he commands, giving you a rough push in the back. You stumble along the corridor trying to formulate a plan of escape. However, the dark hulk of Boris framed in the opening of the tunnel dispels any ideas you had of making a run for it.

'Take care of her,' orders Matt.

Boris picks you up as if you weighed no more than a few pounds and slings you over his shoulder in a fireman's lift. You flail wildly, kicking with your feet and beating with your hands. Boris chortles and enfolds you more tightly in his ape-like grip.

'Scream all you like, young lady,' he laughs. 'Where you are going there won't be anyone to hear you . . .'

Turn to 327

184

'Oh, well. If you really want to go, I suppose I will. I think you're daft, though, to pass up the chance of a good party.'

You have to endure a fair bit of teasing from Penny for the rest of the evening, but on the whole you have a good time at the disco and tumble happily into bed when you get back in the small hours.

Turn to 324

185

Matt raises his eyebrows at your rebuff. His ego has suffered a minor set-back, but he's certainly not going to let it show. You feel the situation has got rather out of hand, and you're also rather uncomfortable about your own behaviour. The only thing you want at this moment is to get back to civilization. Explaining cheerily that you have a mountain of provisions to buy before the shops close at midday, you escape into the sunshine. As you set off down the path you are forced to step aside to let another person pass – a fat man in a dirty lightweight suit.

'Hmm, wouldn't like to meet him on a dark night,' you mutter to yourself, watching him heave his huge bulk up the track. Your distaste turns to disbelief as you see him walk up to the mill and rap on the shutters. Matt certainly has some strange friends.

Turn to 63

186

It is a clear, moonlit night and the island stands stark and black against the silvery shimmer of the sea. There is a fresh breeze blowing and your progress is good. Your arms and legs are certainly very tired by the time you reach the little island, as this is the longest distance you have ever sailed all in one go, but at least you have reached it safely. You leave your board and sail on the little beach, hidden behind a small fall of rocks at one end.

What will you do now?

Make your way up to the temple   Turn to **266**
Head straight for the secret
    tholos   Turn to **116**

187

'Mothers,' mutters Panos with vehemence. 'Mothers are nothing but big trouble.'

You ask him what has given rise to this recalcitrant outburst.

'If you knew my mother,' he raises his hand to

heaven in a gesture of hopelessness. 'She is always trying to interfere in my affairs. "Why don't you give up this stupid windsurfing? Why don't you find a nice Greek girl and settle down? Why don't you help your uncles on the farm? Why do you spend your time with the tourists?" *Panayia mou*, sometimes it is too much . . .'

Thinking it might be a good idea to change the subject before Panos blows a fuse, you ask him about his uncle's farm.

'It is at Paleopoli,' replies Panos. 'At the far side of Simnos. They have several orchards of olives and apricots, many greenhouses . . . and a few sheep. Perhaps you would like to see for yourself? I am going there now to deliver a tractor spare that has just arrived from Athens. Maybe you would like to come along for the ride?'

You have been warned by several people of Panos's reputation, but the invitation does seem enticing. You must make up your own mind.

Will you:

Accept?	Turn to **99**
Decline?	Turn to **165**

188

As you leave the shop, the blistering heat of the near-midday sun hits you and you are relieved to see the bus waiting on the waterfront. The journey is hot and noisy, but at least it is swift, and you are soon back at the villa, helping Penny with the housework.

Turn to 338

189

You can't resist a huge helping of strawberry meringue gâteau. Taking your heaped plate, you slope off guiltily and ensconce yourself in a deep, pink velvet armchair. Nearby, a group of young people are in the midst of an animated discussion. You recognize the most outspoken of them as Liam MacNamara, an Irish archaeology student who is working for the summer vacation on the dig at Aphrodite's Sanctuary. Koutalas, who has put up a large proportion of the funds for the excavations, has invited everyone connected with the project to his party as a token of his gratitude for the work they are carrying out. Liam appears quite heated.

'This project has been dogged by misfortune right from the start. Dr McHenry falling ill, then this new bloke appearing from nowhere to lead the dig. Rumour has it that Koutalas told the authorities he wouldn't put up the money unless they allowed him to appoint the director of operations himself. He's certainly made a rum choice – who is this Dr Orlando Burke anyway? I've certainly never come across his name in any of the journals,' pronounces Liam angrily.

'I'm surprised Koutalas has got the money to finance an operation of this sort anyway,' cuts in a man at Liam's side. 'From what I've heard from various friends in the city, it looks like Koutalas Holdings is heading for the rocks, and I don't think that's just idle speculation.'

The group falls silent at the arrival of an older man with carefully coiffured grey hair, dripping gold chains and clad in a white safari suit.

'Everything to your satisfaction, boys?' he says, raising a full glass of bourbon in a mock toast. 'Bet you haven't seen anything like this before, eh?'

'Yes, thanks, Dr Burke,' answers Liam. 'We're having a great time.'

You watch the safari suit make its way uncertainly towards the bar for a top-up.

If you have recently overheard
   a conversation at a porthole   Turn to 307
If you have not overheard this
   conversation   Turn to 349

190

'Garth!'

'I was looking for you and someone said they'd seen you heading this way. Are you OK?'

You explain about the dress.

'Fine. I'll see you up on deck, then. Come and find me.'

And with that, he retires, leaving you in a bit of a

flutter. The invitation in his eyes was unmistakable. But is this what you want? Unable to think coherently, you concentrate on getting the stain out of your dress.

Turn to 258

191
You find Penny flirting furiously with Lars, and have a little difficulty prising her away. Luckily, she is too preoccupied with her own affairs and plans for meeting the Swede at the disco to pay any attention to your flushed appearance. The rest of the day passes normally and you fall thankfully into bed a bit earlier than usual.

Turn to 346

192
When you reach the crowded waterfront you see Liam MacNamara sitting alone at a table, nursing a bottle of beer, and you decide to join him. Penny goes to talk to Garth Craigmillar at a nearby table. After a few minutes, Liam offers to take you up in the hills tomorrow to see the old ruined fort at Castro. It sounds interesting but do you want to encourage him? You also have to think about your work. If you are going on a day's jaunt, you'll have to ask Penny to cover for you. What will your answer be?

You'd like to go, but you'll
have to talk to Penny first Turn to 224
You don't want to go Turn to 126

193

'Listen sweetheart, it's nothing to do with me. If you want to see this guy Nigel, let him come. If not, tell him to take a jump.'

Well, you had heard about writers being self-centred, but you hadn't bargained for this bald indifference. Matt has made your dilemma seem petty and uninteresting, and you feel childish for not being able to make up your own mind.

Turn to **197**

194

Are the Fates with you? Throw a die.

1–4	Turn to **280**
5–6	Turn to **144**

195

From your rocky vantage point you have a good view of the beach. Panos's next customer is a robust middle-aged German woman. She is having great difficulty in getting up on to the board, but Panos is always near at hand, solicitous and charming. Slithering off the rocks into the sea your foot lands on something sharp and unpleasant. An examination shows that the skin has been pierced by dozens of small black spines. Sure enough, below the surface of the water you see a cluster of sea urchins nestled into every crevice of rock. You attempt to remove the spines that are not too deeply embedded and swim shakily back to the beach . . . trying to remember if the spines are supposed to be poisonous. Limping back along the sand you see Panos coming towards you.

What are you going to do?

Speak first	Turn to **21**
Let him speak first	Turn to **209**

This was a mistake. You meet Donna and she rather pointedly asks you to organize a coffee tray. You do this and take it in to the living room but only have time to discover that the visitor is Garth Craigmillar, who has the other villa at the To Limani inlet, Villa Xanthi, before Donna rather pointedly tells you that she won't need you any more and that you can go to bed.

Seething at being dismissed so summarily, you are about to leave, when Donna's guest interrupts.

'Please don't go on my account. I only dropped in for a moment.'

What will you do?

Stay and risk upsetting Donna	Turn to **252**
Excuse yourself and go up to bed	Turn to **320**

197

All morning you hover by the telephone, nervously picking up the receiver, and then slamming it down before you have finished dialling Nigel's number. You nearly jump out of your skin when towards midday the shrill ring of the phone pierces your eardrums.

'Hi! It's me, Nigel,' says the cheery voice on the end of the line. 'I'm just ringing to check everything is OK for tomorrow.'

Your hesitation means you are now forced to make a snap decision. Will you:

Say everything is fine?	Turn to **343**
Tell him to cancel his flight?	Turn to **211**

198

The track continues to rise and the olive groves gradually give way to scrub. A gentle breeze from the sea refreshes you, though you realize that on a stormy day incredibly high winds must buffet this hill.

'There it is,' shouts Liam. 'That's Castro.'

At first you see nothing, then you realize that the odd-shaped humps ahead of you are moss-covered stones. Angelis settles down for an afternoon nap with the donkeys, while you and Liam head into the old fort.

Turn to 344

199

Gain 1 Luck point.

The motor launch puts on a sudden spurt and swings into the harbour. The driver catches hold of the side of a fishing boat to steady the launch as Matt jumps aboard with one hasty last glance at his watch. He has given you up.

Phew! A close shave.

Turn to 243

200

What will you try?

Knock on the window	Turn to 80
Call for help	Turn to 330
Throw something through the window	Turn to 76

201

Gain 1 Luck point for courage.

'Leave him alone, you thug!' you scream, like a banshee, hoping to scare Fat Man off, rather than tackle him single-handed. To your astonishment, this tactic has the desired effect. Fat Man is keen to preserve an aura of anonymity about his person, and drives off with a screech of brakes, just like in the movies! Safari Suit is still bent double from the blow to his mid-section.

'You OK?' you ask, in your best Starsky and Hutch voice.

'Yeah, yeah, I'm OK,' gasps your lame-dog in distress. 'Huh, how do you like that. Talk about maniac drivers. The guy nearly forces me off the road back there, and when I give him a blast of the horn he drags me outa the car and goes berserk. Some people ought to be locked up.'

Weirder and weirder . . .

When Panos returns, will you tell him about this strange incident?

Yes	Turn to **139**
No	Turn to **53**

202

You walk down a long corridor, trying to find a door that distinguishes itself as a bathroom. After a few minutes, you select a door at random and gingerly push it open. A sumptuous bedroom, but with a bathroom *en suite*. You cannot help having a quick snoop. A dressing-table with a gilt mirror and a set of ivory hairbrushes. Various bits of expensive bric-à-brac. A bookshelf well stocked with holiday reading – Alistair Maclean, a few Maigret novels, a couple of Greek paperbacks, and a whole series of detective novels by a writer called Rex Vitulli. You take one of these books down from the shelf. Scribbled in the front is a message to Koutalas in bold, loopy handwriting: 'To many future ventures, and future successes! Very truly yours, R.'

The handwriting looks familiar, but you can't place it. You replace the book and go into the bathroom to attend to your dress, musing over your find. A few seconds later, you hear the door to the bedroom being opened. You start guiltily. What do you do?

Come out and see who it is   Turn to **190**
Stay put and hope not to
   be discovered   Turn to **318**

Panos looks acutely embarrassed but very relieved that you do not choose to question him more closely.

'Perhaps we can still be friends?' you suggest.

'I would like very much to be your friend,' he grins broadly. 'You are a very understanding girl, and by far the best windsurfing pupil I have ever had.' This is no mean praise coming from Panos. 'Perhaps another day we can go to the island? I know I did promise to take you,' he adds, a note of guilt creeping into his voice.

'Yes, perhaps another time,' you agree, knowing there will be no 'other time'. Ah well, at least you know where you stand now with Panos, but you will have to find another companion for tomorrow's excursion. Looking round the campfire you pick out the shadowy faces of Liam, occupied in incinerating a piece of chicken in the flames, and Matt, deep in some intense discussion.

Who will you approach?

Matt	Turn to 143
Liam	Turn to 347
Neither of them	Turn to 153

204

Donna Chadwick's temper rises a further notch and suddenly a catalogue of other complaints about you and Penny are raging about your head. She even threatens to call Villalink in London to make a formal complaint about you. Things seem to be going from bad to worse. What do you do?

Abandon Donna to stew in her own juice	Turn to **288**
Give in and follow her upstairs	Turn to **84**

205

You leave the path to take refuge behind a low stone wall nearby. Your heart beating wildly and your knees bloody from your speedy ascent of the path, you crouch like a frightened animal, peering through a gap in the crumbling masonry. The voices become louder, but they remain too indistinct for you to pick out what is being said. With wide eyes, you watch as the form of a steely-haired man in a white suite and his balding rotund companion make their way towards the fence. As the latter of the two lifts up the barbed wire for his friend to step through, you notice a distinctive red and green serpent tattoo. You shudder with relief at your close escape.

Do you want to continue?

Yes	Turn to **235**
No	Turn to **293**

206

Luckily you are a strong swimmer but it seems an awfully long way back to the mainland. The currents are strong, the water is freezing, even through your wetsuit and your arms, already tired from the long sail over, are alarmingly weak. However, you are determined to make it somehow

When you are about half-way there, you hear the sound of an outboard motor throbbing through the water towards you. What will you do?

Try to attract the boat's attention   Turn to **216**
Keep quiet   Turn to **276**

207

Gain 1 Luck point. There is fuel in the lighter and it works! You wince as the flame catches your flesh. This is a slow and nerve-racking process, but eventually the ropes are frayed enough for you to wrench your hands apart. You rub your raw wrists and get to work untying the gag around your mouth and then your feet. There is a padlock on the door, but the planking at one side of the hut is fairly rotten. You manage to tear enough of the planks away to crawl out, and stealthily make for the inlet, congratulating yourself on an escape worthy of Indiana Jones. Often in daylight you have boasted that you could swim easily from the mainland to the small island, but in the moonlight the black water looks menacing and unpredictable. Kicking off your canvas shoes, you take a deep breath and plunge in. Slowly you start to swim towards the twinkling lights of Simnos town. You have been warned that the currents in this narrow strait can be treacherous.

How strong a swimmer are you? Toss a coin to find out:

Heads	Turn to **303**
Tails	Turn to **315**

208

Penny looks frankly astonished. Garth merely looks amused at your stammering excuses. Liam barely moves a muscle – certainly gives no sign of pleasure. Could this have been a mistake? In a few moments, Penny stomps off to the disco on her own, saying that she'll meet plenty of friends there. Garth wanders off soon after. Once you're alone, Liam perks up and suggests wandering round the back streets of the town, looking at the less touristy shops, since he wants to buy something for his mother's birthday. The night is still young, the town is alive and bustling, and you feel far from tired. What will you do?

Wander round the town with Liam	Turn to **248**
Go off on your own	Turn to **212**

209

'You should take more care, you know, these rocks are full of *akhinoi*.'

'Full of what?' you ask.

'These things – sea urchins,' he points at your foot which is now beginning to smart with pain. 'Come, let me see.' You try to concentrate on Panos's lecture on the dangers of sea urchins as he grips your foot and prises out the remains of the spines.

Do you:

Take the opportunity to ask
    about windsurfing lessons?   Turn to 5
Offer to buy Panos a drink at
    the beach bar to thank him
    for his kindness?   Turn to 37

210

Your luck is out. You spend a fruitless hour or so trying to hold a finger over the puncture, while paddling with the other hand, but to no avail. Eventually, the dinghy deflates to the point where the water laps over the top and you are forced to swim for it. Unfortunately, you have no idea which way to swim, though you keep going bravely until your strength gives out. Lose 3 Luck points.

A few days later your body is washed ashore on Simnos and the mystery of your death remains unsolved, as does the mystery of Aphrodite's Gold . . .

This is the end of your adventure. Check your score at the back of the book and then try again!

211

Nigel flies into a rage and accuses you of two-timing him. You try to answer his accusations but he won't let you get a word in edgeways.

What will be the outcome of this awkward situation? Throw a die and see if the Fates are on your side.

1–3	Turn to **229**
4–6	Turn to **226**

You pass a pleasant hour or so wandering round the town. However, the small, twisting streets confuse you and in no time at all you are lost.

Emerging into a small square you have never seen before, you pause to take your bearings and are relieved to be able to identify the heavy rock beat from the Black Cat disco. You plunge down another small alleyway, which seems to be leading in roughly the right direction, concentrating on the disco beat.

You are concentrating so hard, that you fail to notice where you are going and run smack into a huge man, who's blocking your path. Fat, ugly and perspiring in the warm evening air, this man has a serpent tattooed on his arm. Have you seen this before?

Yes   Turn to 134
No   Turn to 348

213

You find Liam immersed in a highly detailed conversation with one of the other students on the dig. With some difficulty, you attract his attention and draw him to one side. Once out of earshot, you tell him that you'd like to leave.

'But I can't leave now!' he protests. 'We're reaching a crucial phase on this section and I have to be here to work on it. One of the local boys can take you back. Just ask.'

Rather miffed, you leave him. Sure enough, you manage to cadge a lift back to the mainland and then make your way back to the villa.

Turn to **254**

214

The cool water on your brow is wonderfully soothing and you look up at Liam with a grateful smile. He smiles back and then, on a sudden impulse, swiftly kisses you on the lips. You are startled but find that you quite enjoy the experience. Liam appears to be quite shocked by his daring and leaps to his feet.

'I'm sorry. I just got . . . carried away . . .' His voice drifts off into nothing. How will you reply?

'Don't apologize, I liked it.'	Turn to **322**
'OK, but don't do it again.'	Turn to **6**

Matt springs to his feet. 'OK, if that's the way you want it. I thought we had some kind of understanding between us. I must have been mistaken.' His voice is hard and cold. He refastens the gag around your mouth and leaves you in the dark tomb, grinding the flashlight bulb beneath his heel in a gesture of revenge. You bite back the tears, but a mixture of pride and anger prevents you from begging him to untie you.

Hours later you awake to find Boris and Burke standing over you. Your hands still tied, you are bundled roughly through the bone-strewn chamber, down the passage and out into the night.

'Where are you taking me?' you ask, trying not to let the panic show in your voice.

'You'll soon find out,' says Boris in a voice that chills you to the marrow. 'We'll show you what happens to little girls who meddle in other people's affairs.'

With these words, he picks you up and hoists you over his shoulder in a fireman's lift. You try to struggle but Boris holds you firmly in his gorilla-like grip.

'Careful with her,' warns Burke nervously.

'Shut up and get down to the beach,' barks Boris impatiently.

Burke is obviously the weak link in the trio. If only you could be left alone with him for a while perhaps you could persuade him to let you go. But Boris has other plans in store for you. He hauls you down the beach to a waiting motor launch with Burke at the helm. You are bundled forcibly into the cabin and Boris flings an old wetsuit at your feet.

'OK,' he growls, 'get changed! A little accident has been arranged for you – and it's got to look good!'

The barrel of the mean-looking pistol which he jabs in your ribs persuades you to obey his command. Minutes later he returns, binds you hand and foot and gathers up your discarded clothes. The order to cast off is given and the engine thrums into activity.

Turn to **260**

216

The boat comes closer and closer and you can clearly see that there are several people on board, though you cannot make out any faces. The engine cuts out and strong arms reach down to haul you out of the water.

Are the Fates with you? Throw a die.

1–3   Turn to **120**
4–6   Turn to **334**

217

'Hmm, sounds pretty much like an excuse for shirking all one's responsibilities, if you ask me,' you answer with scepticism. Unperturbed by your criticism, Panos winks cheekily and jumps energetically on the kick-start of his Vespa scooter. The machine roars into action.

'I'm off to deliver some tractor spares to my uncle's farm at Paleopoli on the other side of the island. Perhaps you would like to come along for the ride?'

Whether you find the invitation appealing or not, now you have shown your disapproval of Panos's carefree attitude to life, you would feel embarrassed to accept his offer. Lose 1 Luck point.

Have your movements so far this morning brought you into contact with Matt Jardine?

Yes   Turn to **73**
No   Turn to **165**

218

Unfortunately, you haven't a chance. They are four desperate men and they catch you easily.

Turn to **138**

219

Conveniently, the path further down is flanked by thick gorse and brambles. An excellent hiding-place. You nip behind a dense patch of vegetation and lie flat on your stomach waiting for the men to pass. It takes all your concentration to try to control your breathing which is coming in thick short gasps through fear and exertion. To your utter horror the two men choose to rest on a nearby hillock. You strain to listen to what is being said.

'. . . OK, so we've found what we came for. But that's just the start of our problems. We'll rendez-vous at 3.00 a.m. Tell Rex to make sure the boat is here as planned.'

You raise your head a few inches to watch them go – the slight form of a grey-haired man in a dazzling white suit and his burly companion. The image of a red and green writhing serpent sticks in your mind.

Turn to **235**

220

He turns ugly and gives vent to a cruel little laugh.

'So, Miss High-and-Mighty doesn't like Boris, does she? Well, we'll see about that!'

He makes a lunge for you, but you are lucky and get away. For a moment, it looks as though he's going to follow you and make a horrible scene but one of his mates grabs his arm and says something to him urgently. After casting a glowering glance in your direction, Boris and the others leave. You make your way over to the stage, trying to calm yourself down on the way.

Turn to **310**

221

The midday sun has reached its zenith, its fiery rays beating down savagely on the concrete of the jetty. It's now just past twelve, but still no sign of Panos. You position yourself behind a huge stack of lobster pots and admire the gaily painted fishing smacks with their slender wooden masts and neat little cabins.

The sight of Matt Jardine pacing up and down the harbour, impatiently glaring at his watch, makes you retreat further into your hiding-place. Matt is waiting for the motor launch that will take him out to the party on Koutalas's yacht, and he is expecting *you* to accompany him!

Looking nervously out into the bay you notice that a motorboat has just left the *Hera* and is making its way shorewards. Directing your gaze inland you see the yellow scooter belonging to Panos travelling inexorably towards the jetty.

Which will get to its destination first? Flip a coin and see if the Fates are with you.

Heads	Turn to **199**
Tails	Turn to **295**

222

An understandable decision in many ways. However, it is one that is doomed to disappointment. You are met at the airport by one of Garth's colleagues, who informs you that the whole thing was a plot to get you out of the way. You were becoming too inquisitive about Garth and the mysterious happenings on the island. You now have a depressing future ahead of you. You will have to go home and start looking for another job . . .

Your adventure ends here. You must forfeit 3 Luck points and go back to the beginning. Who can tell what excitements and dramas the future might have held had you remained on the island? Check your score at the back of the book and see if you can fare better next time.

223

'Why don't you make a clean breast of it and admit that you have arranged to spend tomorrow with your girlfriend?'

'I don't know what you are talking about,' replies Panos, deliberately avoiding your piercing gaze.

'So, that dark-haired girl who pops up from nowhere every time we are together is a figment of my imagination?'

'She is not my girlfriend. Our families are connected. We have been friends since we were children.'

'Perhaps you can explain then why your "childhood friend" always looks daggers at any girl who comes within one hundred yards of you?'

Panos is stumped. 'OK. So what if she is my girlfriend?' he admits defiantly.

Infuriated, you give him the dirtiest look you can muster and stomp off to find Penny.

'The trouble with you, Panos,' you shout as your parting shot, 'is that you think all girls find you irresistible. Well, here's one that is going to prove the exception to the rule . . .'

Turn to **133**

224

He looks pleased, and a fleeting smile crosses his lips. You were right. He does look quite nice when he smiles! You ask more more about the old fort but, apart from telling you that it has had a mysterious and violent past, he refuses to give you any details, preferring to let you see for yourself when you go, assuming Penny can cover for you the next day.

Penny eventually returns with Garth in tow and you can see that she is pleased about something.

'Garth has an invitation to join Georgios Koutalas

on his yacht tomorrow afternoon and he's asked us
to come too. Won't it be fun!'

'Who's this Georgios thingummy, Pen?'

'You know! The fabulously rich millionaire who
owns that enormous yacht anchored out in the bay.
Oh, do say you'll come! It'll be a lovely, luxurious
way of spending an afternoon!'

Garth adds his voice to Penny's invitation and
you realize that you have a problem. Do you accept
Garth's invitation and risk upsetting Liam? Or do
you stick to your plan to go to the fort? Which will
you choose?

Go to the fort with Liam   Turn to **170**
Go to the yacht, and put
    Liam off   Turn to **38**

225

Already the beach is beginning to get crowded.
Horizontal bodies in varying tones of brown from
light cinnamon to deep cocoa lie like a shoal of
beached sea creatures, all preoccupied with the
serious business of tanning. Not for the first time
since your arrival you become aware of your own
inferior position in the suntan stakes. Still, everyone
here was this disgusting milky colour once, you tell
yourself encouragingly, gingerly peeling off your
T-shirt. Now for the business of the suntan oil. No
sooner have you completed the tricky task of covering all areas of exposed flesh with Hawaii Coconut
Oil, Protection Factor 3 for skins that tan easily
(well, perhaps a *bit* optimistic), than a short gust of

wind transforms you into a piece of human sand-paper. Muttering through clenched teeth you decide it might be time for your first dip. You have never seen water so blue and clear – except in swimming pools. There are even colonies of minute black fish swimming about. Yes, this is definitely the life!

So as not to appear too pathetic in front of your audience of superior bronzed beings, you plunge athletically into the shallows . . . leaping out again pretty quickly with a sharp intake of breath and many goosepimples. For all its inviting appearance, the sea is surprisingly chilly. Do you:

Stay in the water a while longer?   Turn to **79**

Go back to your beach mat and
   sunbathe?   Turn to **317**

226

'OK then, I'll cancel my ticket!' says Nigel furiously. 'But just don't expect to find me waiting for you when you get back to England.'

You try to think of something to say that will smooth things over between you, but the low humming at the end of the receiver tells you that he has hung up.

You feel guilty that things have turned out this way. Also, a couple of the guests have overheard your heated telephone conversation and this has put you in their bad books.

Lose 2 Luck points.

Turn to **141**

227

You find Penny flirting furiously with a tall, blond Swedish student and have a little difficulty prising her away.

You manage to get a lift back to Simnos with one of the local boys. You wander round the shops on the waterfront for a while before making your way back to the villa.

Turn to 254

228

Matt insists on walking you home to the villa and stays for a drink. You pass quite a pleasant half-hour or so, sipping cognac on the veranda in the sweet dappled light of late afternoon. Suddenly, you feel amazingly sleepy and realize that you will have to lie down. Perhaps you have had too much to drink. Perhaps you have a touch of sunstroke . . . Your last conscious image is of Matt leaning over you, laughing, 'This is goodbye forever, honey!'

The following day, you wake up with a crashing headache and find that Penny is less than sympathetic, since she had to cope with the evening duties all on her own. Apparently, she had tried to wake you, but you were out cold. You guess that Matt slipped something in your drink and you shudder to think what might have happened if you had really managed to make him angry. Lose 2 Luck points.

Later that day, old Katerini comes toiling up the path of the villa, bursting with news of the terrible robbery of temple treasures from the little island. She stays for ages, bewailing the loss, and calling down curses on the heads of the unknown thieves. Unknown, she says – but you know better, don't you? All that fabulous treasure has gone, never to be seen again, and maybe *you* could have done something to prevent it. But it's too late now . . . or is it? Why don't you try again? Check your score at the back of the book and see if you can fare better next time.

229

Nigel refuses to accept any of your reasons why he should not come out to Simnos.

'There's something going on that you're not telling me about,' he snaps angrily at your excuses. 'I'm flying to Athens tomorrow as planned whether you like it or not.'

Turn to **291**

230

Penny chatters away happily as she leads you to the Black Cat disco, perched on a tiny isthmus at the far end of the harbour. At this distance, you can see nothing except the trees, but the heavy rock beat reaches out to meet you and lures you onwards. Suddenly you decide that you are going to enjoy the evening, you relax a bit and start to match Penny's confidences with some of your own.

The heat inside the Black Cat is steamy. Dark shadows mix with pools of bright, flashing lights and the place is packed. Penny sees some friends, and leads you over to a tiny table, where you both squeeze in on an already impossibly crowded bench.

Everyone else at your table gets up to dance, leaving you sitting there. The DJ is playing one of your favourite songs from Duran Duran – a hit you recognize from a few years back. What will you do?

Stay where you are, wishing someone would ask you to dance?   Turn to **86**

Get up and dance on your own?   Turn to **4**

The weather the following day is perfect for your trip to Simnaki. Brilliant sunshine but with a hint of a refreshing breeze.

You wonder how you will get on to the island – the cliffs appear so steep and uncompromising. However, you feel safe in Matt's hands, as he skilfully steers the small craft around the far side into a shallow inlet between the rocks. He appears preoccupied and reluctant to enter into conversation.

'Are you interested in ancient history, Matt?' you ask, attempting to break the uneasy silence.

Matt pushes back his sandy forelock with his sleeve, and puts his head on one side as if to consider the question.

'I'm more interested in what happens to people now than what happened to them in the past,' he replies after a pause. 'What good are fragments of priceless mosaic to all the thousands who don't have a dime to their name? . . . But I'm sure Liam will step in and give you a full guided tour of the ruins if you're interested,' he adds with a teasing wink.

The boat secured, you begin the tortuous ascent to the Sanctuary. It's a difficult climb, but Matt is there to lend a gallant hand when the going gets tough. Reaching the top you collapse exhausted. Not too exhausted though to appreciate the splendour of the marble ruins of the Temple of Aphrodite which rises majestically before you.

Turn to 241

232

Luckily, you are a dab hand at motorbike engines, having had an old wreck of your own back in England, which you renovated and then sold. For some inexplicable reason, the moped has developed an air-lock in its fuel system. You siphon off enough fuel to deal with the problem and then fix the pipes back together again. There's still no sign of Liam, so you have a short rest and a drink of lemonade to take the taste of petrol out of your mouth. As you sit there, you hear the sound of another motorbike – a much more powerful machine than your little moped – coming up the hill. To your surprise, the bike doesn't appear on your donkey track and, as the deep engine note dies away up the hill, you realize that it must be travelling up a path roughly parallel to yours. Someone going up to inspect a far-flung olive grove – or someone heading for the old town? You have no way of telling. Just then you hear the pop-popping of Liam's moped and wave to him as he appears at the top of the hill. You restart your bike and go up to follow him again.

Turn to 142

233

'Sabrina, my darling, I have brought you your idol,' says Koutalas, proudly displaying his protégé to a group of frighteningly sophisticated young women who resemble a colourful *Vogue* centrespread. Sabrina, a svelte German girl in an emerald green silk sheath dress, embraces Matt like an old friend.

'Ah, Georgios, you have made my dream come true. But who could have guessed that my favourite author would turn out to be such a handsome hunk of a man.'

Sabrina's friends are anxious to muscle in on her act, and the group closes around her and Matt, relegating you to the sidelines.

'Matt, Matt, you must sign this copy of your book for me,' croons a striking redhead. As she shoves past you her glass of pink champagne neatly decants itself on to the skirt of your white dress.

Feeling angry and rejected you go in search of some water to sponge out the stain.

Turn to 39

234

Not that he needed much encouragement. His lips are warm and tender and, as his arms tighten around you, your heart pounds. A long, pleasurable time passes until, with a start, you remember Penny. But before you can go and find her, Garth says that he has a proposition to put to you. What could it be? Perhaps things are going too fast for you – do you wish to hear it?

Yes   Turn to 158
No   Turn to 304

235

The path dips into a hollow clearing. It looks as if excavations have been taking place here as well. On further investigation, you realize that what you have stumbled across is another of Liam's underground 'beehive' tombs, set apart from the rest, about 600 metres west from the main temple. You hesitate at the entrance to the tomb and wonder if you have the guts to go in by yourself. Just then your foot hits something lying on the ground. Bending down you pick up an expensive-looking crocodile wallet with 'RV' initialled in gold leaf on one corner. You take the wallet back into the sunlight and open it up. Credit cards belonging to one Mr Rex Vitulli . . . some Greek money . . . and a season ticket to the Museum of Modern Art in New York. A fuzzy black-and-white photograph of the cardholder stares up at you. The quality of the snap is poor, but the likeness unmistakable. It's Matt Jardine!

Shaken, you wonder what your next move should be. It's very dark in the tunnel . . . Are you the Girl Friday type who never goes anywhere without a flashlight? Toss a coin to find out.

Heads   Turn to **125**
Tails   Turn to **263**

236

You pop in to see how the guests are getting on. Old Mrs Chadwick seems to have gone to bed and those who stayed in are just sitting quietly reading or playing cards. You tell them where to find tea and coffee in the kitchen in case they want a late-night drink and then slowly make your way out to the annexe. Just as you reach the back door you hear Donna Chadwick answer a knock on the front door. You run back down the corridor.

Turn to **196**

237

The lever operates a hidden trap-door leading to an underground vault. Unfortunately, any treasure it might have once contained has been ransacked.
Lose 1 Luck point.

Turn to **45**

238

Something prevents you spilling the beans to Garth. He looks at you as though he is about to pump you further and then visibly changes his mind. Your conversation moves on to more neutral topics until you reach the jetty on the other side. Garth seems to have no real desire for your company for the rest of the afternoon, so you wind your way back to the villa. The rest of the day passes in a bit of a haze until you finally take your exhausted body to bed.

Turn to **346**

239

You find yourself wandering dreamily around the cloisters, imagining how many monks through the centuries had walked upon these smooth stone slabs, heads bent in prayer.

Suddenly something leaps out at you from behind a pillar. You scream and jump backwards. Standing before you is a little wizened old monk with bright beady eyes and wild grey hair.

'Aphrodite, Aphrodite!' he warbles ecstatically, grabbing you by the arm. '*Ella, ella,* come . . .'

It seems that he wants you to follow him. Ah well, what harm will it do. Anyway, you can't really tell a monk to get lost. You follow him up a stone stairway into a large room full of dusty glass cabinets of uninteresting-looking relics, each carefully labelled. The room is encircled by a gallery which houses a library of huge leather-bound volumes that look as if they could house the contents of the *Encyclopaedia Britannica* several times over. The mad monk leads you on a tour of inspection, chattering all the while in Greek. Eventually he takes you to a corner of the gallery and carefully pulls down one of the weighty tomes from the shelf. He opens the page at a drawing of a statue of a goddess.

'Aphrodite,' he croons lovingly. '*Orea.*'

'Yes, very beautiful,' you comment encouragingly.

'*Orea* . . . beautiful,' he repeats, and points to the picture and then to you.

Oh no, he seems to think you are some incarnation of the Goddess. He then turns to the back of the volume where you see he has made a secret pocket by carefully glueing the back pages to the cover. He taps his nose secretively and extracts from the pocket a piece of fine vellum. It appears to be some kind of map – the map of a classical temple by the look of things. Outside its perimeters are a group of roughly sketched circles.

Then something catches your attention. A symbol. The same symbol you have noticed in varying forms all over the island – on the local pottery, the jewellery, even the home-spun fabrics. The emblem is imprinted upon a solitary circular shape at the western corner of the map. Your friend is now suffering transports of glee over this little revelation. Placing his finger over his lips he indicates that this is to be a secret between the two of you. Meticulously he replaces the vellum in its hidey-hole and thrusts the book back on to the shelf.

You are just wondering how to make your get-away when the door to the museum flies open.

'Adelfe Vangelis!' calls a stern-looking young man. From his dress and his age you guess he is a postulant. You decide you don't like the look of him. Poor old Brother Vangelis looks like a child who has been caught with his hand in the sweetie jar.

'I hope my brother hasn't been too much of a nuisance,' smiles the young man smarmily. 'We generally try to keep him away from visitors. He is, as you have probably gathered, quite insane.'

Turn to 273

240

Your Luck is out. The dogs resist your friendly advances and drive you back down the path, snapping at your heels. Lose 1 Luck point. At the end of the path they give up and lie there panting, watching you as you wind your way back towards the town. You have to do your shopping.

Turn to **55**

241

The dig is not remotely how you imagined. The ground within the site has been neatly divided into regular sections with pathways in between for access. The work looks slow and painstaking and is carried out with trowels. Every so often a wheelbarrow passes between the sections gathering any finds that have been unearthed, and taking them off to the site hut where they are meticulously cleaned with a toothbrush, labelled and photographed. It doesn't look much fun to you.

'Disappointed?' Liam asks, a trifle dejected.

'The dig doesn't look quite as dramatic as I antici-pated . . . but I'm sure it's very interesting if you know what's going on,' you reply, trying not to hurt his feelings.

'You can't really appreciate the importance of the work we are doing here unless someone explains it to you. Let me give you a proper guided tour of Aphrodite's Sanctuary. There'll be a few surprises you weren't bargaining for. I can promise you that.'

Who did you come with?

Penny?	Turn to **325**
Matt?	Turn to **31**
Liam?	Turn to **105**
Garth?	Turn to **261**

All the mopeds in the hire shop have seen better days but you choose the two that seem to be in the best working order and set off along the road out of town, with the engines spluttering and giving off huge clouds of blue smoke. Eventually, they seem to settle down and you cruise along at a steady 50 kilometres per hour. Soon after you leave the last outskirts of the town behind you, Liam leads you off along a broad dirt track on the right. The ground rises steeply ahead of you and the path narrows quickly. The little mopeds pound up the hill in low gear but it takes all your concentration to keep the moped steady and on course. Liam's moped is raising clouds of dust ahead of you, which doesn't make things easier.

You follow Liam as he takes several different tracks, each one getting steeper and more difficult to navigate. The moped engines are labouring in bottom gear now. Suddenly, your moped coughs once, twice and then stops altogether. You try to restart it with no success. You shout at Liam to stop, but by this time he's too far ahead to hear you and carries on round the bend and out of sight. What now? Do you wait for Liam to come back, or do you try and see whether you can fix the moped yourself?

Wait   Turn to **16**
Try to fix the moped   Turn to **124**

243

The yellow scooter skims over the potholes, jarring you into the saddle. Involuntarily, your arms tighten around Panos's slim waist as you meander your way through cool groves of swaying bamboo and orchards of lemon and olive trees. Lining your route are tall clusters of prickly pear – huge cactus-type plants bearing bizarre orange fruits. After about

twenty minutes you reach a crossroads with a sign-post. One arrow points east, the other west. Upon each are written the same words:

Monastiri Aghios Dionysus 5 km.

You are baffled. Panos explains that there are two approach roads to the monastery, the westerly road goes along by the coast, the easterly road is the mountain route.

Which way do you want to go?

Along the coast	Turn to **319**
Through the mountains	Turn to **267**

244

Not bad. One of the dogs calms down but then the other sets him off again. They look increasingly nasty. Lose 1 Luck point. Will you risk another guess?

Hermes and Zeus	Turn to **340**
Apollo and Icarus	Turn to **162**
Go home instead	Turn to **312**

245

If over the past weeks you have got to know Panos quite well and he has expressed a romantic interest in you, then he is likely to be annoyed at you asking his advice on your relationship with another boy. If you haven't got to know him, you shouldn't be asking his advice anyway.

Turn to **197**

246

Are you going to be lucky to get away without trouble from him?

Are the Fates with you? Throw a die.

1–3	Turn to **220**
4–6	Turn to **72**

247

The weather the next day is perfect for your trip to Simnaki, brilliant sunshine with a hint of a refreshing breeze. Garth's Zodiac inflatable dinghy has an outboard motor that reduces the journey across the strait to a matter of minutes.

He isn't being very friendly this morning. It occurs to you that perhaps you have brought him here against his will. Perhaps he had other plans for the day, but was too polite to refuse your request? You voice these impressions as he is helping you out of the dinghy on to a rocky plateau some feet above the water. You feel his grip tighten. When you are standing level he does not release you, but fixes you steadily with his warm brown eyes. His face creases into a grin.

'Don't be silly,' he scolds. 'How could I refuse an invitation to spend a day in your company? Besides, who would protect you . . .'

'From what?' you ask, trying to keep your voice steady.

'From everything,' he answers enigmatically.

Turn to **241**

Away from the tourist trap of the waterfront, the back streets of Simnos are bustling with life, and you spend a pleasant hour walking around.

Eventually, your wanderings take you past the Post Office, and you decide to see whether there are any letters for you. There aren't. As you turn to leave, you bump into Matt Jardine coming into the Post Office. A few minutes later, you see him emerge from the building again, clutching two envelopes, which surprises you, since there were no letters addressed to him in the Poste Restante box when you looked. You mention this to Liam and are surprised to see his mild face harden with suspicion.

'There's something funny about that man,' he says. 'He's supposed to be here writing a great novel, but he spends all his time lounging around in bars, or staying on Koutalas's yacht out in the bay. I've seen him sniffing around the dig over by Aphrodite's temple, too. Local colour, *he* called it!'

You laugh and accuse him of having a devious mind. After all, you point out, Liam clearly also harbours suspicions about Garth Craigmillar.

Liam just grunts and, in his curt manner, offers to take you home. Will you walk back to the villa with him, or would you rather carry on walking round the town on your own?

Go home with Liam	Turn to **118**
Walk round on your own	Turn to **212**

249

Panos has just collected a tractor spare from the Post Office that he must deliver to his uncles' farm at Paleopoli, a hamlet on the far side of the island. He is going by bike, and suggests you might like to come along for the ride.

You have heard dubious reports of Panos's reputation, but having agreed with his philosophy that you should live for the moment you feel you cannot back down now. You clamber on to the back of his beaten-up Vespa scooter and sling your bag across your shoulder.

'Ready?' Panos turns to you, smiling.

Ready or not, the next minute you are hurtling out of town following the tortuous ascent into the mountains. You grip Panos tightly around the waist and hope for the best.

Turn to **137**

250

Penny isn't the only pretty girl attempting to lionize Matt. As you reach him, a gorgeous blonde successfully persuades him to sign her book for her. As she gazes at him adoringly, he inscribes the book to her with his love, handing the book back to her with a speculative look in his eyes. He holds her hand longer than is strictly necessary and you get a definite impression that an invitation has been made and accepted. Penny greets Matt and launches into a long, involved and embroidered tale of your adventures with Garth's dogs. At the mention of Garth's name, Matt's face hardens, but Penny doesn't appear to notice.

Just then, the blonde squeezes past you and jogs your elbow, spilling some of your pink champagne down your front. It makes a nasty stain on your new white dress. Penny stops her yarn and helps you try to mop it off with a napkin, to no effect. You decide that you must go and sponge it thoroughly, or the dress will be ruined. Excusing yourself, you hurry off to repair the damage.

Turn to 48

251

The Black Cat is bursting at the seams tonight and Jason, the West Indian DJ, is in his element, his long dreadlocks drawn back in a jaunty pony tail, putting his audience through their paces with a punishing volley of singles. The night is close and the dancers are starting to wilt under the relentless glare of the lasers. Sensing that a change of tempo would not go amiss, he puts on a slow number and the dancers come together with their partners. You sit back in your seat and listen dreamily.

'Like to dance?' Panos offers you his hand.

Trying not to look too chuffed at being singled out by one of the best-looking men in the disco, you follow him on to the dance floor where you sway in rhythm to the fluid melodies of Lionel Ritchie. As the last refrain dies, Panos leads you back to your seat.

'Listen, I have to go now. I must help my mother at the hotel.' So one dance is to be your allocation for the night. Too bad. Panos senses your disappointment. 'But tomorrow is your day off?' You nod. 'I am also free all day tomorrow. Maybe you would like to see some more of the island . . . we could take my scooter and make a day of it . . . visit the monastery of Aghios Dionysus, stop off for a swim at Souli perhaps . . . What do you say?'

This seems an excellent way to spend your day. You and Panos arrange to meet at midday at the harbour. Panos leaves and you are joined by Penny and a couple of American girls she has befriended.

Penny's friends are rather overpowering and you excuse yourself on the pretext that you want to ask Jason for a request. As you approach the DJ's console you try to melt back into the crowd when you see that Jason is deep in conversation with Matt Jardine. Too late, Matt has spotted you and comes after you. He appears to be in a contrite mood after his behaviour this morning.

'Hey listen. I'm sorry if I came on a bit strong

earlier on today. No hard feelings, eh? Anyway, by way of atonement I'd like to invite you to be my guest at the party on Koutalas's yacht tomorrow.'

You are completely taken aback by the invitation.

'Ah, I can see what you are thinking,' laughs Matt. 'How does somebody like me get invited to the yacht of an international shipping magnate? Well, the invitation is a genuine one. If you want to put it to the test, meet me at the jetty at midday. There'll be a motor launch to pick us up and take us out to the *Hera*.'

Walking home you consider your dilemma. What should you do tomorrow? Go with Panos as planned, or follow up Matt's invitation?

If you decide to opt for Panos's
   invitation   Turn to 221
If you would prefer to accompany
   Matt to the party   Turn to 161

252

'That's kind of you,' you say with a smile, trying to ignore Donna's disapproving frown. 'I'm new here, and I'd love to know more about the island.'

A strange look crosses Garth Craigmillar's face swiftly and then it's gone, leaving you wondering what you had said to make him react that way.

'Oh well, I don't know much about the island, I'm sorry to say. I've been keeping pretty quiet up at the villa. Don't see anybody much.' He looks a touch embarrassed. 'I really only called to ask whether I could use your phone. Something's come up in the

States and it's too late for the phones in town.' He looks at you inquiringly.

Before you have a chance to answer, Donna gushes, 'Of course you can. Anything we can do to help.' Her guest seems to have made quite an impression on her and you quickly look over to her husband Steve to see what he's making of her performance. Luckily, he doesn't seem to have noticed.

The telephone is in the annexe, just outside Penny's room, and is not normally available for the use of the guests unless there is an emergency. All calls have to be recorded in the phone book and paid for. This is a dilemma. Donna had absolutely no right to offer the phone to Garth Craigmillar, but in refusing his request you are bound to appear churlish. It would help put Donna in her place, but might alienate this rather attractive stranger.

What do you do?

Offer to show him the phone   Turn to 114
Say he can't use it   Turn to 166

'Charming,' you mutter under your breath, peeved at Koutalas's blatant disregard for you.

'Yes, isn't he,' echoes a voice behind your left shoulder – Garth Craigmillar. A friendly face – what a relief. Garth has come to the party alone because Penny, who was to have been his guest, is laid up with a violent attack of too much sun and *moussaka* – much to her rage and disappointment.

'What do you think of our magnate then?' he asks.

'I think he's odious,' you answer without hesitation.

'I think you might have made a very correct assessment of his character,' laughs Garth. A current of sympathy passes between you. Compared to Matt, Garth seems so open and uncomplicated. He takes a glass of pink champagne from a passing waiter and hands it to you. Unfortunately someone jogs your elbow as they are walking past. You and Garth both look down to see a rose-coloured stain seeping through your white dress. Garth makes a brave attempt to mop it up with a table napkin, but you must go and sponge the stain thoroughly with water or the dress will be ruined. Excusing yourself, you hurry off to repair the damage.

Turn to **39**

254

Late that afternoon, old Katerini, from one of the nearby cottages, comes breathlessly up the path to the villa, bursting with news. There has been a terrible robbery of temple treasures from the little island! She stays for ages, bewailing the loss and calling down curses on the heads of the unknown thieves. Unknown? She may not know who they were but you might have some suspicions. Perhaps you came close to being involved. But it's too late now. Lose 3 Luck points and try again! You can check your score at the back of the book and see if you can fare better next time.

255

'Not as fit as you thought, eh?' Matt Jardine draws level with you and smilingly offers you his arm. 'The path gets even steeper from now on. Allow me to offer my assistance.'

For the first time you get a good look at him. He can't be more than twenty-three or twenty-four, but his cool self-assurance belongs to someone who has already made his mark on life. He is deeply tanned with wild sandy-coloured hair, rather too long to be fashionable.

Trying not to sound too out of breath, you give your most patronizing smile and say, 'I think I can just about make it on my own, thanks all the same.'

Matt is obviously not going to give up so easily.

'Well, I've always admired self-sufficiency in a girl. I suppose it must keep you in pretty good shape, rushing round after all those creeps at To Limani day and night.'

'How do you know I work at the villa? And anyway, what do you mean "creeps"?'

'Oh, I've caught sight of you plenty of times since you arrived, busily going about your domestic chores. I was hoping you might catch sight of me and I would have the opportunity to introduce myself. Now it seems my wish has been granted. And come on – don't pretend you feel any loyalty towards that crowd of package-holiday philistines?'

'Not everyone has the time – or inclination – to spend their summer playing Robinson Crusoe, you know,' you retaliate smartly.

Matt grins lazily, 'Ah, so you've taken the trouble to find out a bit about me as well. Not such a cool customer as you make out, are you?'

You search frantically for an appropriately cutting response but, with an infuriatingly confident smile, Matt swiftly takes his leave and strides off up the path, leaving you struggling behind.

Vowing to get your own back you retrace your steps to the villa.

Turn to **320**

256

Unfortunately, your escape is discovered almost immediately by the three left in the *tholos* and they chase after you. You rush headlong down the path towards the beach and almost into the arms of the fourth man.

Turn to **62**

257

Hello again!

Still no letter from you, but I expect it's the post. Anyway, no more need to write now, I'm coming out to Greece! I know you'll be surprised by this, but I was on my way to work this morning and I thought, 'Why not?' I've got enough saved for the fare, and presumably you could find me some cheap accommodation for one week in the village? I'm flying out on Wednesday 14th to Athens, I'll catch the midday boat from Piraeus, so I should be with you sometime early evening. I'm sure I'll find the villa quite easily.

See you soon!
Lots of love,
   Nigel

Turn to 135

258

Just then, two people seem to come to a halt just under the bathroom porthole. By the tone of their voices, the conversation hasn't been all that amiable. A snatch of it floats through to you.

'Let's just say that it would be to your advantage to speed things up a bit.' This voice is deep and menacing. You may have heard it before.

'It's not like digging up potatoes, you know. Things have to be taken slowly. It's a delicate operation.' This voice is new to you, a grating voice, with an American accent.

'And Rex. He's a co-operative workmate?'

'He'll do. He's so desperate for cash, he'll do anything we ask him.'

You creep closer to the porthole in the hope of catching sight of the two men. They have their backs turned to you, but the one closest to you has a distinctive tattoo of a twisting serpent on his arm.

The men move off and you wait until you feel the coast is clear before leaving the cabin. Where do you go now?

Up on deck   Turn to **294**
Back to the party   Turn to **30**

259

Panos is now stomping up and down like a spoilt child, cursing the gods for his misfortune. You point out tactfully that his energies might be more constructively employed in helping you wheel the scooter off the road into a nearby field where you can get to work on repairing the puncture. It so happens that you have often watched bike-mad friends tinkering with their machines, and from what you have gleaned, mending a tyre is mostly down to common sense. There are some tools in the rear panier and you issue Panos with instructions to fetch further materials from the village you passed a few kilometres back. He looks most taken back by this command, especially coming from a *girl*.

'But what do you know about bikes?' he protests.

'Considerably more than you do by the look of things,' you retort matter-of-factly. There's no answer to that one. Panos slopes off sheepishly on his errand, leaving you to tackle the flat tyre.

Motorbike mechanics is extremely hot work. Having skilfully removed the offending tyre, you can get no further until Panos returns from the village. So, plucking a few figs for provisions, you go and recline amongst the bamboo. You'll have to be careful not to doze off because the spot where you are lying is completely hidden from the road, and Panos might think you have been kidnapped! Despite your resolution, it only takes a few minutes for you to start drifting into semi-consciousness until the sound of a car pulling up at the side of the road jolts you back to the land of the living, and you peep out to see who it is. The door swings open and the driver steps out. His elegantly coiffured, steel-grey hair makes it difficult to guess his age, but you assume him to be no more than thirty-five at the most. He looks very out of place on the dusty highway, clad in an immaculate white safari suit. Seconds later a grey saloon pulls up alongside. The driver of the second car is quite a different kettle of fish . . . heavily built with a Mediterranean equivalent of the great British beer gut, balding, with thick rubbery lips and a jowly face, translucent with grease and perspiration. If you recognize him a shudder of terror runs through you. A dark shadow runs the length of his left forearm which you suppose to be a tattoo. The first part of their conversation is obscured by the sound of a crop sprayer flying overhead, but whatever has been said can't have been very friendly because Fat Man is now shoving Safari Suit in a most anti-social manner. Safari Suit swats him away feebly and dusts down his white jacket as if to prevent any risk of contamination.

'OK, OK,' he says to Fat Man, 'tell him I get the message. But he'll have to wait. There are one or two youngsters who aren't as green as the rest. If they get wind of what's going on behind their backs, then we'll all be heading for the cooler and that means the boss too, *and* his precious protégé, Rex Vitulli.' It seems that Fat Man doesn't like the sound of this by the way he grasps Safari Suit by the collar and pulls his face up to his own.

'You know, Burke, one thing that our employer really dislikes is threats. You of all people should know that he is a great believer in honour amongst friends. And you know that to betray one's friends when the going gets tough is a very, very dishonourable thing to do. Wouldn't you agree?'

Fat Man obviously feels that Safari Suit might need a little persuading on this matter and pinning him to the bonnet of his red sports car he administers a thudding blow to his stomach. Safari Suit cries out and creases up in pain.

Do you:

Rush out of your hiding-place and intervene?	Turn to **201**
Stay put and wait until Panos arrives back – which should be any time now?	Turn to **117**

260

The launch heads out for open sea for some time and the swell gets stronger. After about three-quarters of an hour, Matt comes into the cabin, hauls you to your feet and takes you out on deck. Dawn is rising but the gentle flush of pink on the horizon is the only thing to be seen. You are out of sight of land. With very little ceremony, Matt and Orlando Burke drop you over the side of the launch, into an inflatable dinghy.

'Koutalas would kill us if we turned up with you in tow,' Burke explains. 'This way you should be able to make your way back to land eventually but not until we have made good our escape!'

You plead with them but your entreaties fall on deaf ears.

'You'll be OK. Sure you will,' says Matt as he casts you off.

Boris appears on deck in time to hear this and repeats Matt's words, though with a heavy hint of sarcasm. '*Sure* you will!' His laugh has an ominous ring to it.

As the launch speeds away from your dinghy, you notice that the fading sound of the boat's engine gives way to a noise that sends shivers of horror running up and down your spine. There's a sharp hissing to your right! The dinghy has been punctured just above the waterline and the precious air which keeps you afloat is escaping! Could this be what Boris meant?

How lucky are you?

If your Luck score is less than 10	Turn to **54**
If it is over 10	Turn to **210**

It looks like Garth has vanished into thin air. You tell Liam you'll be back in a minute and do a quick inspection round the site. Maybe he's gone into the hut. You poke your head round the door.

'Looking for something?' asks a tall Nordic-looking boy who is fastidiously employed in cleaning a shard of pottery with a fine cloth.

'Some*one*, actually,' you reply. 'Have you by any chance seen a tall English bloke with light brownish hair wearing a stripy T-shirt and cut-off jeans?'

'You mean Garth, yes?' answers the boy. Registering your surprise, he explains that he knows Garth quite well because he often comes out to the island to look around. 'He's quite interested in ancient history, isn't he?' he says.

'Is he?' you reply, with barely concealed astonishment. You have to admit that if ancient history is one of Garth's great passions, he has certainly never let on about it.

'Oh yes,' the boy goes on. 'He seems very knowledgeable. He was even able to give us some interesting advice on the classification of a few pieces we were having some difficulty identifying. Anyway, the last time I saw him he was heading off towards the other side of the island. Be careful though. There is some land subsidence over there. The terrain is very unsafe.'

You thank the boy and go to find Liam. Well, if Garth wants to wander off on his own, let him.

Turn to **105**

After a frustrating half-hour or so, Liam gives up in disgust. There's nothing you can do to fix the moped. You can't leave it there, so you have no choice but to walk it back to the town. After an argument in the hire shop, you get your money refunded, and you agree to have another go sometime in the future. Irritated at the waste of an afternoon, you bid Liam goodbye and go back to the villa. Lose 1 Luck point.

Turn to **47**

You turn on your flashlight and tread warily down the dark musty tunnel, not knowing what lies in wait for you at the end. You make a concerted effort to push all thoughts of skeletons and corpses to the back of your mind, but Liam's words keep echoing in your head: '. . . so economical space-wise . . . existing skeletons moved to one side . . . tomb reopened and more bodies buried alongside . . .'

After what seems like an age you arrive in the vaulted chamber with its domed ceiling. Nothing could have prepared you for the awful vision of death and decay before you . . . Shattered remains of skeletons, fragmented by the passing of centuries and armies of greedy vermin and insects. A wave of nausea sweeps over you and for a minute you feel you are going to faint.

The sound of scuttering nearby brings you back to your senses. The thought of lying here in this vault with rats crawling over your unconscious body makes you determined to keep your wits about you. Crawling through a narrow opening from the main vault, you find yourself in a small chamber. Fortunately, there are no more skeletons here.

It appears to be empty, but something tells you that if the treasure exists the clue to its whereabouts lies in this room. Looking around, you notice three things: a broad ledge, about two metres from the ground, running along the far wall; a large slab of jutting stone in one corner; a metal lever hidden amidst the rubble covering the floor. Which will you choose to investigate?

The ledge	Turn to **101**
The lever	Turn to **237**
The stone	Turn to **89**

264

Neither Garth nor Liam wants to accompany Penny to the disco, so she stomps off crossly on her own, claiming that she's meeting friends there anyway. Garth too says he can't stay, but offers to walk you home, since he's going your way. Liam says he's going to wander round the back streets of the town, as he's got to find something to send his mother for her birthday and he fancies that the less touristy shops might be away from the main streets. The night is still young, the town is alive and bustling, and you feel far from tired. What will you do?

Go home with Garth	Turn to **68**
Wander around the town with Liam	Turn to **248**
Neither of these	Turn to **212**

265

The passage to the tomb smells dank and unappealing. It looks as if it could house all manner of nasty creepy-crawlies. You explain to Liam that you are prone to attacks of acute claustrophobia and would prefer to give this subterranean exploration a miss. Liam is disappointed at your lack of enthusiasm, but does not press you. As you re-emerge blinking into the bright sunlight a young woman struggling with a wheelbarrow full of earth calls out to Liam to come and lend a hand. Liam politely excuses himself and rushes off to her assistance.

Have you had enough of ruins for one day?

Yes	Turn to 293
No	Turn to 269

266

You make your way silently up to the temple, confident that the noise of the wind in the trees will hide the sound of your footsteps. The tall, ghostly columns of the ruined temple cast long deep shadows across the scarred area of the dig and you wait carefully in the gloom beneath a nearby olive tree, watching for any movement. Suddenly, your eye is caught by a glimmer of light from the little wooden hut that serves as an office for the dig. In the next moment, it has gone. What will you do next?

Creep over to the hut	Turn to 316
Leave and head down to the *tholos*	Turn to 116
Wait a bit longer	Turn to 28

267

Your chosen route winds upwards through parched hills and stunted olive groves planted on amazingly inaccessible slopes.

But why is the scooter making that unhealthy spluttering noise, as if it has contracted a bad dose of bronchitis? Panoo pulls up at the side of the road, and if his volley of expletives are anything to go by, the damage looks pretty serious. In true dramatic style, your companion delivers a furious kick to the front mudguard, and sits down upon a handy milestone, head in hands.

How do you fancy doing a spot of motorbike mechanics?

You must be joking!   Turn to 337
You don't mind having a go   Turn to 15

268

A gap-toothed individual, who goes by the unlikely name of Angelis, agrees to take you up to Castro on his donkeys. Liam leaps efficiently into the saddle of his animal, but you find the oddity of the traditional Greek saddle a bit much. Angelis helps you up with rather more enthusiasm than is strictly necessary and Liam recommends you to ride side-saddle, the Greek way.

Travel by donkey has its advantages but speed is not one of them. You make a leisurely progress out of town and then take to the donkey tracks leading up to the old fort. It certainly is a peaceful way to spend an afternoon. Liam and Angelis practise speaking Greek and English respectively and there is nothing for you to do but to sit swaying dreamily on top of your donkey as it plods up the path.

Suddenly, the peace is shattered by the roar of a motorbike coming up the path behind you. Angelis tries to manoeuvre the donkeys to the side of the path, but he's too late. As the motorbike thunders past, your donkey panics, screams and gallops headlong down through the olive groves, with you clinging on for dear life.

Are the Fates with you? Throw a die.

1–3	Turn to **18**
4–6	Turn to **100**

269

You feel a bit superfluous wandering amongst all these people engaged in serious toil. Perhaps you should go off on your own and explore the island.

You are at present standing in the centre of the main temple's foundations. Which way will you go?

North	Turn to **113**
South	Turn to **83**
West	Turn to **77**

270

Garth seizes the now rather soggy wad of papers with a cry of triumph.

'Well done! You've got the one thing I was sure we'd be too late for. Real, documentary proof, which ties the whole bunch of villains in together.' He runs a quick eye over the rest of the papers and gasps as he reaches the bottom one. 'And this is invaluable! This is a list of Koutalas's contacts who "fence" the stolen treasures!'

You feel too exhausted to take much of this in. You are just happy to stand and watch as the police round up Matt, Burke, Boris and the rest. Gain 5 Luck points.

Turn to **350**

271

A lucky escape! Gain 1 Luck point. You have managed to get out of what could have been a nasty situation, but next time you'll have to keep your curiosity in check.

Scurrying down the path, you are forced to step aside to let another person pass, a fat man in a dirty light suit. He eyes you suspiciously, his breath rasping with the exertion of the climb. 'Hmm, wouldn't like to come across him on a dark night,' you mutter to yourself, watching him heave his huge bulk up the slope. Where can he be going? He doesn't look like a farmer, and he's certainly not out for a stroll. You look on in surprise as he walks up to the windmill and raps on the shutters. Matt Jardine certainly has some unappealing friends.

Turn to **63**

Your luck is in. They search for you furiously without any success. Once or twice they come breath-stoppingly close but do not see you. Eventually, Matt says crossly that they will have to go back to loading the treasure, otherwise they will miss the pick-up time. As soon as they are gone, you make your way down to the beach, aiming to take your sailboard back to the mainland and alert the police. Unfortunately, as soon as you put the board into the water, it begins to sink and you realize that the villains must have discovered it and holed it to prevent you getting away. You have no choice now – you will have to try to swim for it.

Turn to **206**

273

You find Panos sitting on the battlement chatting to a pale young man dressed in frayed khaki army shorts that hang loosely on his spare frame and a faded Cambridge University T-shirt. It's Liam, the student archaeologist.

'Hello – taking time off from the dig?' you ask breezily.

'I just had to get away for the day,' replies Liam glumly. 'Things are lousy at the moment. Morale is really low. But actually I spend a lot of my free time up here.'

To cheer him up you recount the story of your experience with the mad monk.

'Ah, Brother Vangelis,' laughs Panos. 'He's quite a character. He used to be a well-known archaeologist in his time. Before he went completely crazy, of course!'

'Shame,' mutters Liam. 'He could have been useful in tracking down a few clues.'

'Clues?' you and Panos echo in unison.

Turn to 3

274

A brief look of disappointment crosses his face but he doesn't press you further. It's a pleasant walk back to the villa, and you do your best to try to discover more about him. However, he skilfully evades all your gentle probing and, when he leaves you at the villa door, you are none the wiser.

Turn to 324

275

You find Garth taking detailed snaps of the dig with his little pocket Olympus. He seems quite happy to leave when you suggest it.

Back on the mainland you buy him a drink in one of the waterfront bars, by way of a 'thank you' and then make your way back to the villa.

Turn to **254**

276

You bravely turn your back on the boat, knowing that you are less likely to be spotted that way, and tread water gently as the boat comes closer. It roars past you in a matter of seconds and you have to struggle to keep your head above water as the boat's wake crashes over you. As soon as you are sure it is well out of sight, you start swimming again.

Turn to **315**

277

'I suppose I just wanted to see you, Matt.'

His expression softens.

'. . . but then I lost my nerve when I heard you coming back.' It seems that flattery has got you out of a tricky situation. Matt is satisfied with your explanation and asks you in for a drink.

'I'm sorry I lost my cool back there . . . the thing is, I'm rather sensitive about privacy. Can you understand that?'

You nod mutely, wondering where the conversation is leading. Matt seems intent on continuing his lecture.

'You see, in my profession, it is essential that I have no distractions when I feel the urge to work. And that means a definite *no* to uninvited guests.' He pauses and moves close until his disarming cobalt eyes are only inches from your face.

'Even if they are of the attractive, female variety . . .'

Do you:

Stand still?	Turn to **17**
Move away?	Turn to **185**

278

Rather surprisingly, Garth doesn't put in an appearance after lunch as arranged. After a short wait, you and Penny decide to walk up to his villa, expecting to meet him on the way down. There's no sign of him on the way, and you begin to worry that he might have forgotten all about you. His villa, too,

looks suspiciously quiet, though undoubtedly
attractive. After a small hesitation, you and Penny
walk up the little path that leads to the villa's front
door.

Suddenly a furious barking breaks out and two
large black dogs hurtle out of the shade on the
veranda and bar the path in front of you. They look
vicious and resist all your friendly overtures. The
only way you will calm them down is if you call
them by name. Do you know what they are called?

Hermes and Zeus	Turn to 340
Apollo and Hermes	Turn to 244
Apollo and Icarus	Turn to 162
No idea	Turn to 104

Hermes and Zeus Turn to 340
Apollo and Hermes Turn to 244
Apollo and Icarus Turn to 162
No idea Turn to 104

279

'Matt!'

''Fraid so. You should have kept your infernally
prying nose out of my business and perhaps we
could have stayed friends. As it is, I'm going to have
to tie you up for a while to keep you out of trouble.'

A second flashlight in the chamber reveals two
more shadowy figures.

'Help me tie her up, Boris,' orders Matt.

As Boris thrusts you roughly on to a stone slab
and secures your wrists, you notice the serpent
tattoo. The other man seems more squeamish.

'Who are these people, Matt?' you ask, hysteria
rising in your voice.

'Oh, I'm so sorry,' apologizes Matt with great
sarcasm. 'How remiss of me. Allow me to introduce

you. Orlando Burke, eminent archaeologist, and Boris, faithful bodyguard of Georgios Koutalas.'

Conversation is put to an end by a piece of material that is tied tightly around your mouth.

'Sweet dreams, honey,' crows Matt. 'And don't wait up for me. I'll be back late tonight!'

With peals of laughter ringing in your ears, you watch the three men disappear into the darkness, leaving you alone with the stench of decay and the scurrying of rats.

You wake from a fitful sleep what you assume to be some hours later. It takes you a few seconds to remember where you are and the desperate nature of your situation. At least Matt had the humanity to leave a flashlight so that you are not enshrouded in total darkness, but how long will the battery last? Grim thoughts of being buried alive in this hell-hole creep into your mind. But what's this? A light in the next chamber.

'Hi!' Matt shines a torch in your face. He then bends over and removes your gag. Your mouth is sore and dry.

'What time is it?' you ask, trying to sit up.

'About six o'clock,' he replies.

You point out with satisfaction that everyone will be searching for you by now. They'll have realized something is up. Matt informs you that this technicality has been taken care of. He has told your friends that you met some people down on the beach and have decided to accompany them to a fiesta in Laki, a village some five kilometres from

Simnos town. The note of triumph has now faded from Matt's voice. Could he be regretting his involvement in this skulduggery?

'Here, I brought you some water. It might be a long night,' he says, lifting a bottle to your lips.

Do you:

Spit the water in his face?   Turn to **311**
Drink the water and thank him?   Turn to **67**

280

It is a long, terrifying drop but your dive cuts the surface of the water perfectly and you are soon swimming strongly out to sea. Something stings your cheek sharply and you realize that Burke must be firing at you. You try to swim under water as far as you can and, when you surface, the shooting has stopped. Perhaps you are now out of range.

Turn to **206**

281

Your getaway seems to be going to plan until the sound of raised voices draws you from the cabin, where you have been snatching a few hours' rest, on to the deck. Immediately you spot the large motor launch moored alongside the boat you realize with a sick feeling what has happened. Burke, Boris, Matt and the captain are lined up along deck, their hands raised over their heads, under the surveillance of a stern-looking police commander – whose men have already set to work, methodically searching the boat for contraband. You have stumbled, quite by misfortune, into a coastguard vessel on a routine patrol. Little do they realize the value of the haul they have intercepted. Lose 5 Luck points.

Your adventure ends here. If you are lucky you will get off lightly with a warning. If you are not so lucky you might end up in a Greek jail for your part as an accessory in this caper.

Check your score on at the back of the book and try to be wiser next time round.

282

You fall heavily and bang your head against the hut. Shaken and stunned, you don't have a chance to move before a heavy hand is laid on your shoulder and drags you to your feet. You have been caught by Orlando Burke!

'Oho! A snooper, eh? Well, you'll soon find out what we do to snoopers!' he snarls.

Turn to **138**

283

Matt's second caller of the morning is an obese, surly-looking man in a soiled lightweight suit and open-necked shirt. Judging by the rivulets of perspiration working their way downwards from his high shiny forehead to his quivering jowl, the climb up to the windmill has been rather too much for him. Matt's welcome is curt and formal. They exchange a few hushed sentences in Greek. Matt's growing unease is evident from the awkward glances he shoots in your direction. Sensing that you are no longer welcome, you excuse yourself on the pretext that you have urgent errands to run. Hurrying back to the cheerful hustle and bustle of the harbour, your mind brims with unanswered questions . . . What sort of person is Matt Jardine? And what bizarre bond links him to an unsavoury individual like that?

Turn to 63

284

Your luck is out.

Turn to 102

The lighter stubbornly refuses to spark. Lose 1 Luck point. In a fit of frustration you fling this useless object to the floor and break down in floods of angry tears. Gradually your sobs subside as you drift exhausted into a deep, dreamless sleep. When you come to, bright sunlight filters through the crack in the splintered wood. You can hear voices outside. In a desperate bid to attract attention you fling yourself at the door.

'Seems to be someone inside,' observes a strangely familiar voice. 'Someone give me a hand to break this padlock.'

In a matter of seconds the door flies open to reveal the sturdy form of Garth Craigmillar and a squad of uniformed policemen.

'What on earth? . . . We thought you'd been kidnapped,' says your rescuer, amazed.

As one of the policemen unties you, you explain briefly how you happen to be in this extraordinary situation. Garth nods gravely at your story. There is something about his manner that has altered, although you can't quite put your finger on it.

'We've been on to this racket for quite a while,' he admits when you have finished. 'We've now got Koutalas in custody, but of course there's no real case against him unless we can recover the haul before it leaves the country. Shame you couldn't have given us the tip-off before you got yourself taken prisoner,' he concludes, with a trace of a frown that makes you feel rather crushed.

But wait a minute, why is Garth involved in this

business anyway? You feel you might be due an explanation. Garth looks slightly embarrassed at your question.

'Ah, sorry. Allow me to introduce myself properly.' He flashes a card in front of your eyes. Underneath his photograph you glimpse the typewritten words: *Commander G. M. Craigmillar, British Intelligence*.

Your adventure ends here. But where is Matt now, and where is the treasure? Could you have done something to prevent Koutalas's scheme from succeeding? There are still a lot of questions left unanswered. Check your score at the back of the book, then start again, and see if, by taking a different route, you fare better next time.

286

'Good. You'll have fun, and you'll also be able to see what old Koutalas is like. Oh, by the way,' he says, as a bit of an afterthought, 'that writer who's camping in the old windmill, what's-his-name . . .'

'Matt Jardine?'

'Oh yeah, Matt Jardine. He's likely to be on the yacht tomorrow – always has been every time I've been there. I reckon he must know Koutalas well.'

You try to find out more about Matt as you walk home with Garth, but he skilfully evades all your gentle probing and, when he leaves you at the villa door, you are none the wiser.

Turn to **324**

Slamming the shutters closed, you slump down on your bed, burying your face in the coolness of the pillow. Forty winks and you'll be ready to tackle the next chore – getting the supper ready.

Startled, you sit bolt upright. Someone has been watching you. At the side of your bed stands a pale, blond-haired youth in running shorts and T-shirt.

'Sorry to make you jump like that,' says Greg, 'I just felt I should come on a peace mission on behalf of the Chadwick family. Donna's a bit het up after the journey. The kids drove us all bananas on the boat . . . Fancy a drink?'

Do you:

Politely turn him down, explaining
   you have to start the supper   Turn to **299**
Say, 'I'd love one'   Turn to **335**

288

An understandable move but, in the long run, a mistake. Deprived of an audience, Donna lashes herself into a real storm and makes good her threat to call head office in London. How much of her complaint they believe is uncertain but eventually you will receive a stern letter from your boss, reminding you that the care of the Villalink guests is your prime concern, however unreasonable their demands may seem at times. Lose 2 Luck points.

For the moment, you push this unpleasantness to the back of your mind and go off in search of Liam.

Turn to **60**

289

Penny refuses to see Nigel's imminent arrival as a problem. On the contrary, she suggests that his presence on Simnos will make you appear more desirable in the eyes of any other admirers you may have, and even if you and Nigel don't hit it off, there are plenty of other distractions to occupy him for the week. Besides there is always the possibility that absence will have made the heart grow fonder and your reunion will be a pleasant one.

Turn to **197**

290

Just as you drift off to sleep, you see a strange light winking from the windmill up on the headland and wonder what it could be. Perhaps a kind of lighthouse? Though you'd expect the beam to be steadier than that. Perhaps someone was signalling out to sea? Then you see an answering light on the little island of Simnaki across the narrow strait.

Turn to 32

291

Aphrodite, Goddess of Love, is not feeling generous towards you at this point in time. In fact, things seem to have gone extremely sour in your life. Nigel's visit turns out to be a catastrophe. Shunned by Matt, silently scorned by Panos, abandoned in your hour of need by Penny and Garth, you seem to have taken a nosedive in the popularity ratings. Nigel is pleading with you to give up your job and come home with him, and you are being plagued with phone calls from your mother also demanding your return. Finally, you submit to pressure and contact Villalink to say that you are resigning due to family problems.

Your adventure ends here. You must forfeit 5 Luck points and go back to the beginning.

Who can tell what excitements and dramas – romance even – the future might have held had you remained on the island? Check your score at the back of the book and see if you fare better next time.

292

If you made an arrangement to
   meet Liam   Turn to 78
If not   Turn to 332

293

Who did you come to the island with?

Matt   Turn to 345
Penny   Turn to 227
Garth   Turn to 275
Liam   Turn to 213

294

You find Garth alone, up on the top deck, looking out towards the small island. As you join him, your bare arms touch and a tingle of excitement runs through you. He turns towards you with a warm look in his eyes. Do you want to encourage him to kiss you?

Yes   Turn to 234
No   Turn to 88

295

The motorboat engine appears to have cut out. The driver climbs into the back of the boat to examine the outboard motor. Panos rides on to the jetty, ignoring Matt who is casually striding up and down with his jacket slung over his shoulder, whistling a jaunty tune as if he hasn't a care in the world. You have no choice but to emerge from your hiding-place. Matt and Panos both smile expectantly at your sudden manifestation. However, Matt's expression soon turns into a scowl when he sees you climb on to the back of Panos's scooter.

'I thought we had a date this afternoon,' he growls. You explain with embarrassment that you have made a double booking. Matt is fuming. Panos is loving every minute of this confrontation but is trying not to look *too* smug over his victory.

Matt could be the sort to bear a grudge. Lose 1 Luck point.

Turn to **243**

296

That does it. Burke's nerve cracks and he rushes out of the hut gibbering with fright, making a dash for the path down to the secret *tholos*. Realizing that he may be back soon, you enter the hut and grab up the remains of the paperwork he left scattered by the little stove. Then you knock the stove over, deliberately setting fire to everything else on the table. You want to be sure that if any of the villains return, they won't realize that anything is missing. Satisfied with your handiwork, you leave the hut and make your way cautiously down the little path to the secret *tholos*. Gain 2 Luck points.

Turn to **116**

297

Panos has been promising to take you over to Simnaki to visit the temple of Aphrodite since your arrival, but for one reason or another, the trip has always been postponed. Now seems as good a time as ever to try to pin him down and make him keep his promise. However, when you suggest windsurfing over to the island the following morning, Panos becomes cagey and mutters that he has made other arrangements that he cannot cancel.

Do you:

Be discreet and drop the subject?	Turn to **203**
Provoke an argument?	Turn to **223**

298

You both cautiously creep into the tunnel, feeling your way carefully. To your alarm, the passage narrows considerably and the only way forward is to crawl. Are the Fates with you? Throw a die.

1–3   Turn to 52
4–6   Turn to 336

299

The bustling daytime hubbub has been absorbed by the twilight, and only the rush of the evening wind in the olive and bamboo groves and the faint thrumming of the crickets disrupts the silence that has spread over To Limani.

You help Penny clear the remains of the dinner from the long trestle table which stands under an awning on the terrace and carry them into the kitchen. Now you are alone, Penny is eager to give her run-down on the guests.

'Don't mind those two couples from Sussex but I'm not too keen on the Chadwicks. Well, Steve seems OK, but Donna . . . she's going to be the difficult one, I can see it. Greg seems a nice sort of bloke – not very dishy though . . . Mind you,' she continues, 'there's a couple of local characters worth a second glance.' She pauses, waiting for some expression of interest on your part. Failing to obtain any encouragement, she prattles on regardless. 'There's our next-door neighbour at the Villa Xanthi for a start. Garth Craigmillar – he drove past us in his white jeep yesterday. Dead nice looking – not very sociable though. He came up here about a week ago to ask if he could use the phone, but he didn't hang around. Now Matt's a much better bet . . .'

'Who's Matt?'

'Matt Jardine. He's from New York. Actually, he's quite a famous author. He camps out in the derelict windmill at the top of the donkey track. God, you should see it . . . what a mess! He's here for the summer to write a new novel, but he says he's got writer's cramp.'

'You mean writer's block, don't you?' you suggest.

'Something like that . . . anyway I'll introduce you. You'll see him around, he's the rather scruffy, eccentric-looking guy with sandy-coloured hair.'

Feeling the need for a change of subject, you ask Penny if there is somewhere on the island you can learn to windsurf. Penny rolls her eyes with relish.

'There certainly is. Better be careful though in case you fall into the irresistible clutches of Panos Pavlides. He runs the windsurfing school down on the main beach, and he's absolutely gorgeous, but does he know it! Of course, he's been trying to chat me up since I arrived, but I just tell him to get lost!'

She wipes her hands and takes off her apron. 'There, all finished. I'm off to the Black Cat for a bop. Coming?'

What do you want to do?

Go to the Black Cat?	Turn to **230**
Stay in and get an early night?	Turn to **10**
Go for a walk?	Turn to **111**

300

Matt insists on walking you home to the villa and stays for a drink. You pass quite a pleasant half-hour or so, sipping *retsina* on the veranda in the sweet dappled light of late afternoon.

After your first drink, Matt offers to fix you one of his special Martinis, which sounds fun. However, he has a slightly strange look in his eye when he returns with the drinks and, after one sip, you decide not to risk it. You take the opportunity of tipping most of the drink into one of the tubs of flowers on the veranda when Matt's back is turned and then feign sleepiness. You are rewarded by an almost wolfish look of pleasure on Matt's face as you peep at him through your eyelashes, and you keep up the act until he has carried you to your bed.

As soon as he has gone, you sit bolt upright and try to plan your next move.

Turn to 346

301

Quite right! What do any of these people know about your relationship with Nigel? It is even possible that one or other of them might have a selfish motive in advising you to act in a certain way. Nigel's imminent arrival is *your* problem and you must make up your own mind how to cope with it. You have reacted wisely so far. Gain 1 Luck point.

Turn to 197

Trying to encourage him, you say that you'd love to know more about the island that is to be your home for the summer.

He tells you a queer story about some legendary treasure which is supposed to be hidden somewhere on the little island of Simnaki across the strait.

'That's fascinating,' you say. 'Have you found anything yet?'

'Not much. There's very little to see there. Just a few broken pillars and white, stone remains in amongst the grass and the scrub. What was left of the temple has virtually disappeared, and I don't imagine that we'll discover anything startling.'

Feeling a bit disappointed, you silently promise yourself a trip over to the little island with the tragic past, sometime soon.

You stay chatting to Liam for quite a time. For all his untidiness and abrupt way of talking, he is pleasant company. Eventually you realize that it has got very late and, after a swift look in at the disco, you decide to leave Penny to her own devices and make your way home to bed.

Turn to **320**

303

Gradually you feel yourself winning against the current and the shoreline begins to draw closer. You swim into a deserted cove and sit shivering on the beach wondering what to do next. You could go to the police, but you have no concrete proof that the treasure exists, or that Matt and his gang are planning to make off with it. Besides, it's unlikely that the Greek police are going to listen to the seemingly crazy hunches of a tourist. The best thing to do would be to lie low for a few hours, then return to the island and catch the tomb-robbers red-handed. But where should you hide? You come to the conclusion that the villa is probably as safe as any hideout since it's probably the last place your enemies would think of looking, and even if Matt did discover you had escaped and came after you, it would be practically impossible for him to abduct you in front of the guests. Anyway, you are tired and soaking wet, and in need of a good bath. Sneaking into your room by the back stairs you decide not to confide your adventures to Penny – this is one mystery you are determined to solve alone.

Turn to 346

304

The sound of a 'proposition' is going a lot too fast for you. You've enjoyed your interlude with Garth, but don't intend taking it further. At least not yet. You need time to think.

Turn to 30

'What sort of books do you write?' you ask over a glass of warm beer.

For someone who had just spent the last few minutes lecturing you on his need for privacy, Matt seems curiously ready to talk about himself.

'Well, I suppose you could say I've made my name in the blockbuster league. You know the sort of thing . . . international locations, industrial espionage, hi-tech gadgetry . . . I suppose *Catapult* is my best-known work . . . ah, I see a glimmer of recognition . . .'

'Of course I've heard of *Catapult*. I saw the film starring Donald Sutherland. I thought it was very good.'

'But now I'm working on something different. Something I've been wanting to do for ages – a stab at serious fiction.'

'What's your theme?'

'I'm not altogether sure myself at the moment! It seems to be about how people compromise themselves in order to survive . . . and what happens to those who don't.' He laughs at your blank look. 'The scenario is quite interesting though. The action takes place on a Greek island.' He moves his hand across the table and places it firmly on top of yours.

Do you:

Meaningfully withdraw your hand?	Turn to **185**
Leave your hand where it is?	Turn to **17**

306

Penny pouts and stamps her foot crossly.

'Oh, honestly, you're such a goody two-shoes! You're daft to pass up the chance of a good party – and for a bunch of fuddy-duddies.'

Stung, you answer hotly that since Villalink have seen fit to send you, and her, to Simnos to care for the guests and pay you for doing so, you feel honour bound to do the work.

Penny flushes angrily, but before she can retort, Garth takes the wind out of her sails by explaining that he was planning to get you both back on shore in plenty of time to get back to the villa and prepare the evening meal. Penny is visibly disappointed but you shoot Garth a grateful look, which he returns with a smile.

Gain 1 Luck point.

'Won't you change your mind and come to the party tomorrow?' he asks.

Well, will you?

Yes	Turn to **38**
No	Turn to **2**

307

Why should that grating American voice seem familiar to you? You know for certain that this is the first time you have set eyes on this man. Then a half-remembered snatch of conversation comes back to you: 'It's not like digging up potatoes you know . . . he's so desperate for cash he'll do anything.'

Of course, one of the men at the porthole was none other than Dr Orlando Burke.

Turn to **349**

308

You have had plenty of time to think up a reasonable story, but you have an awful feeling that Matt isn't convinced by it.

Are the Fates with you? Throw a die.

1–3	Turn to **228**
4–6	Turn to **300**

309

You slip through the barbed wire and scramble down the bank. It strikes you as strange that a section of land that has been fenced off in this way should have such a well-worn path. There's obviously something odd going on here. Could the dig be a front for some shady dealings? The sound of voices makes you stop dead in your tracks. Something tells you that whoever your fellow trespassers are, they are not going to be overjoyed to meet you.

Which way will you go in search of a hiding place?

Up the path   Turn to **205**
Down the path   Turn to **219**

310

The tiny stage to one side of the disco floor is stacked high with speakers and flashing lights, at the centre of which is the DJ, seated behind his control desk and mike. Behind him, you can see a vast library of singles and LPs, which is manned by a tall, slim bloke with dark, wiry hair and spectacles. You ease yourself up on to the stage and ask whether you can have a request played for you. The DJ smiles, doesn't say anything and points to his friend, before turning back to the desk to croon something into the mike.

'Don't mind Jason,' his friend says a bit nervously. 'He's into the cool-cat DJ image at the moment. You should see him breakdancing! My name's Liam. How can I help you?'

You spend a pleasant half-hour or so, talking to Liam, with Jason butting in between records before you get back to the question of your request, which Jason eventually plays, while you dance with Liam. After a bit, Liam announces that he's hot and is going to have a walk outside. Do you want to join him?

Yes   Turn to **150**
No   Turn to **98**

'OK, if that's the way you want it,' says Matt in a peculiar voice, completely devoid of emotion. 'Just remember, you got yourself into this. Small fry don't matter one bit to us, and nothing, but nothing, is going to stop us now we've come so close.' He roughly reties the gag around your mouth and backs through the narrow opening into the next chamber.

'Boris wanted to get rid of you right away, you know . . . maybe I shouldn't have stopped him . . .'

You lie in the horrible darkness (Matt has taken the flashlight with him) paralysed with fear, trying to ignore the scurryings of the rats, and wondering if this could all be some terrible nightmare. Eventually, the sound of footsteps and a bobbing beam of light announces the arrival of Boris and Burke. Boris unties your bonds and pushes you roughly through the passage.

'We thought you might like a change of scenery,' he chortles nastily, and picks you up in a fireman's lift.

'Careful, Boris,' warns Burke, a note of uncertainty in his voice.

You struggle wildly and pummel Boris with your hands, but to no avail, this man has the strength of an ape.

What horrible fate lies in store for you?

Turn to 327

312

Furious with the dogs and disappointed to have your afternoon spoiled, you head off to your villa. Still no sign of Garth. Eventually you give him up and go down to the beach, where you spend a pleasant time windsurfing and sunbathing until it is time to come home.

Turn to 47

313

The interior of the yacht looks more like a mansion than a boat. Only the portholes give it away – but you wouldn't be surprised to find French windows leading on to rolling lawns and flower beds. The main reception area is furnished in dusky pink with thick cream carpets. A bold selection of modern oil paintings line the walls. The best of Greek and international cuisine is arrayed on tables covered with white damask tablecloths – whole fresh Scotch salmon, mountains of black caviar nestling in beds of crushed ice, giant silver platters of seafood – king prawns, scallops, succulent oysters with shells the colour of slate. Expressionless white-gloved waiters circulate amongst the guests with silver trays on which are balanced glasses of pink champagne.

Your eyes skim the sea of faces. One face that does look familiar – and surprisingly at home in these luxurious surroundings – is that of Garth Craigmillar, looking appealingly enigmatic in a pair of very dark glasses and a beautifully cut cream linen suit.

You and Matt fill your plates from the buffet and are just settling down to the serious business of eating when your host arrives on the scene, a stocky man in his late fifties with craggy, weather-beaten features.

'Matt, how delightful that you could tear yourself from your great work for a few hours to grace us with your presence,' crows Koutalas without the slightest note of sincerity in his voice. 'And what a charming little companion you have found for the occasion . . .' He holds out a stubby hand in your direction. Before you can reply he turns again to Matt.

'I have some people who are dying to meet you and receive their personally signed copies of your latest book. Come.'

Do you:

Tag along behind?	Turn to 233
Discreetly melt into the background?	Turn to 253

314

You are only just in time. Burke's launch is just putting to sea as your boat arrives. A searchlight snaps on from the top of the police boat and, after a desperate struggle from the thieves, the police succeed in boarding. Matt, Burke, Boris and the rest are taken into custody, while you take Garth below and show him the temple treasure. Luckily, none of it appears to be damaged. Gain 3 Luck points.

Turn to 350

315

The sea is rougher than you realized. You battle against the current but it insists on pulling you sideways. After fifteen minutes your destination seems to be getting no closer, and you begin to panic. A sudden gust of wind sends a wave crashing over you. You thrash around in terror, crying feebly for help, but knowing there is no one to hear you. Finally, you give yourself up to the current. A few moments later you have lost consciousness. Lose 5 Luck points. Your adventure ends here.

Check your score at the back of the book, then go back to the beginning and try again.

316

You make your way over to the hut, dodging quietly from shadow to shadow. When you get there, you edge round to the small window at the side and peer in. At first you can't see anything, but then you see a definite glimmer at one end of the hut and alter your position so that you can see more clearly. Unfortunately, you slip on some loose rubble as you move and fall awkwardly.

Are the Fates with you? Throw a die.

1–5   Turn to **160**
6   Turn to **282**

Once again you embark upon the laborious task of covering yourself from head to foot in suntan oil and lie back to soak up the heat. In the distance you can hear someone shouting instructions to a novice windsurfer.

'Must remember to ask about lessons,' you mumble to yourself. The beach noises seem to be getting more and more distant, the lapping of the waves settles into a vague murmur, the Greek music from the beach bar no more than an indistinguishable hum . . . you start to drift off into oblivion.

OUCH! You open your eyes with a start, spitting sand out of your mouth.

'Can't you watch where . . . ?' Your sentence is lost as you look up to see a pair of sturdy brown legs . . . red swimming trunks . . . a tanned, muscled torso . . . strong arms carrying the colourful sail of a windsurfer. Looking down at you apologetically are the darkest eyes you have ever seen, framed by a messy halo of charcoal black curls. A silver identity bracelet winks at you in the sunlight. A single word is engraved across it: PANOS.

Do you:

| Give him a piece of your mind? | Turn to 145 |
| Wait for his apology? | Turn to 29 |

318

Whoever it is only seems to pop his or her head round the door and then leave again. You stay frozen for a few minutes after you hear the outer door shut again, just to make sure you are alone. Then you relax.

Turn to **258**

319

You look down dizzily at the aquamarine water and the deserted, white sandy beaches hundreds of feet below. Enraptured by the breathtaking scenery and the heady scent of the flowering hibiscus and lemon groves, you rest your head on Panos's powerful shoulder. He turns briefly and smiles at your gesture of affection. At that moment a large blue and white bus with Greek music blaring from its windows looms before you round the bend. Luckily Panos's reflexes are sharp and he manages to slam on the brakes before you career over the cliff edge. There is a loud bang as the bike swerves into the side of the road. You both dismount to assess the damage. Panos swears loudly as he prises a large nail out of the fast deflating front tyre.

'Puncture,' he says.

How do you feel about a spot of motorbike mechanics?

No thanks. You'd rather leave that
  sort of thing to the boys   Turn to **337**
You don't mind having a go   Turn to **259**

320

You fall into bed gratefully and think back on the day's events. You feel a bit sad and doubtful about this huge plunge you have taken, and wonder whether you have made the right decision. Briefly, you realize that you are missing Nigel – safe, comfortable Nigel – but then give yourself a mental shake. You're going to enjoy this job and it's going to be a real adventure for the first time in your life!

You're still not sleepy, tired though you are. What will you do?

Read the little book on the history of Simnos	Turn to **132**
Turn out the light and lie gazing at the stars	Turn to **290**

321

'Don't hurt me!' you scream in panic.

Matt is alarmed by your hysterical outburst and relaxes his grip on your arm.

'You work at the villa with Penny, don't you?'

Trying to regain your composure, you reply sheepishly, 'That's right. I've been hearing so much about you from Penny I thought I would call in and introduce myself whilst I was up this way. The door was open so I walked in. Then I panicked when I heard you coming back.'

Matt is satisfied with your explanation – not to mention flattered at the thought of you and Penny discussing him at length over the washing up. He asks you in for a drink.

What do you say?

'I think I've presumed on your
  hospitality enough for one day.
  Maybe another time.'   Turn to **271**
'That's very nice of you. It'll
  give me a chance to show you
  that I'm not really a hardened
  criminal!'   Turn to **305**

322

He kisses you again, only for longer. All your
bruises are forgotten in his arms and it is only when
Angelis returns, leading your runaway donkey,
that you break apart. There's more to Liam than you
thought.

There's a brief discussion about whether you feel
strong enough to carry on up to the old town, which
you end up by saying you feel fine. You all have a
brief rest and then set off again.

Turn to **198**

323

Perhaps you did not inspect the contents of the box as thoroughly as you supposed. Anyway, you don't feel like making an issue of it.

Coming into the harbour you are assailed by a yellow tornado – in the form of an extremely flushed and excited Penny, bursting with news.

'You'll never guess what,' she squeaks. 'I've been invited on board Koutalas's yacht by Garth Craigmillar! Apparently, Garth's company did some big promotion for one of Koutalas's companies and they are *great* buddies. There's a really glam party on the boat tomorrow, and I'm going as Garth's guest. What do you think of that?'

Without waiting to hear your reaction she rushes off to tell anyone else she can find.

You and Matt stare out to sea, where the imposing white stern of the *Hera*, Koutalas's massive luxury yacht, is anchored in state.

'Would *you* like to go aboard her?' asks Matt.

'Fat chance,' you laugh.

'I could invite you, if you wanted to go,' says Matt in his coolest voice.

'Oh yes,' you answer mistrustfully, 'and how do you plan to organize that?'

'The trouble with you is you're much too cynical. I may look like a beach bum, but you forget that in the great wide world I am actually quite an established author with one or two blockbuster bestsellers to my name . . . you'd be quite surprised at the people I know. Anyway, if you are interested in taking me up on my offer, meet me on the jetty at midday.

There'll be a motor launch to take us to the yacht. You can wear something casual – it'll be an informal affair.'

Leaving you to ruminate on this extraordinary invitation he goes off to challenge a group of fishermen at a nearby taverna to a game of backgammon.

Turn to 35

324

The following morning passes swiftly and soon you and Penny are free to prepare for your afternoon's expedition. Where are you going? You can change your mind if you want to.

To Koutalas's yacht	Turn to 278
To the old town	Turn to 22

325

You can't very well abandon Penny – after all you were the one to suggest this trip. Where can she have got to? At last you find her, drinking Coke behind the site hut, talking to Lars. By the look of things they are discussing more than the structure of Doric columns and metopes. Perhaps Aphrodite's power lingers on amongst the ruins? Who knows? You discreetly disappear and rejoin Liam.

'OK, Liam. Surprise me,' you command.

Turn to 105

326

Much as you resent doing this, it does eventually calm Donna down. When she's finally satisfied, you are free to find Liam and go off to the old town.

Gain 1 Luck point for keeping your temper with a guest.

Turn to **60**

327

You are taken to a broken-down shepherd's hut, which, from the sound of the crashing waves, you suppose to be on the cliff top. The hut is dark with an earth floor, but at least there are no rats or skeletons. Through a splintered slat in the wall you can glimpse the moon. It looks like Matt and his cronies are planning something big tonight, but you are the only one who could stop them, and you are powerless. You slump on the floor despondently. How could a harmless trip to Aphrodite's Sanctuary have led you into such danger. You know the 'old' Matt would never have harmed you, but this 'new' Matt that seems to have taken over seems capable of anything.

You sit on something uncomfortable and fish around to see what it is. It's a cheap plastic cigarette lighter. You try to think how you could use this object to your advantage. Then you remember something . . . an old detective film you once saw on the television, where the hero was held captive, and managed to burn through the ropes securing his wrists with his cigarette lighter. It's going to be tricky because your hands are tied behind your back and you can't see where you are aiming the flame. But first of all, let's see if the lighter has any fuel left in it.

Are the Fates with you? Throw a die.

1–3   Turn to **285**
4–6   Turn to **207**

328

It is touch and go but you make it finally, with your arms and legs shaking weakly, you drag the board and sail up the beach a little way and then hide them behind a small fall of rocks at one end. After a long pause to compose yourself, you think about the best place to start your investigation.

Up at the temple?   Turn to **266**
At the secret *tholos*   Turn to **116**

329

Your hesitation has cost you dearly. Lose 1 Luck point. An angry shout alerts you to the fact that your getaway has been foiled. Picking yourself up you attempt to limp to safety. Matt runs out and grabs you roughly by the arm.

'OK. Suppose you just tell me what your game is,' he hisses, his usual carefree grin having been replaced by an expression that could almost be described as sinister.

You say the first thing that comes into your head. What did you do last night?

If you walked along the cliff path   Turn to **277**

If you stayed in or went to the
   disco   Turn to **321**

330

As Burke comes to investigate your cry, you get a sinking feeling that things aren't going to be quite that simple. Try as you might, you can't think up a sensible story to explain your presence there and you try to get away. Unfortunately, he is too quick for you and you are caught.

Turn to **138**

331

'You're the one who ought to be the writer!' exclaims Matt. 'You've got the most vivid imagination of anyone I know. Listen, there's nothing sinister about Koutalas, or his methods. He's just a very clever operator, and naturally he's got plenty of enemies. As for Liam's half-baked yarn about treasure . . . you can put that down to the fact that he's concocted a theory about the Sanctuary, and now he's determined to make reality fit with it.'

Perhaps you have let your imagination run away with you. You are beginning to feel a bit stupid at having confided your 'discoveries' to Matt.

'Anyway, you don't want to worry too much about legends of the past,' he goes on, the cynicism fading from his voice. 'There's too much to enjoy in the present.'

Turn to **169**

332

You dress silently, taking care to choose dark clothes and soft shoes. You creep out of the villa and make your way swiftly down to the beach. Panos's little hut is locked but you remember seeing where he hid the key the last time you were here and soon have a sailboard out on the sand. You borrow one of Panos's black wetsuits, lock the hut again, and take the board out to sea.

Are the Fates with you? Throw a die.

| 1–3 | Turn to **92** |
| 4–6 | Turn to **186** |

333

Tonight you have been invited to an impromptu beach barbecue in one of the small coves dotted around the bay. A bonfire has been lit and you recognize several people you know in the glowing firelight, Matt and Liam amongst them. Panos too is gracing the party with his presence, having coasted into the bay with characteristic panache on his windsurfer! With Panos's coaching you yourself have become fairly expert at this sport over the last few weeks, but the idea of putting yourself at the mercy of wind and current in the darkness of the night seems foolhardy to say the least. Out to sea, the dark, jagged silhouette of Simnaki watches over the bay. You have made up your mind that tomorrow you will spend the day there. Your curiosity has been whetted by the myths and legends concerning the small island, but you have still not had the opportunity to see its ruined temple for yourself.

You glance about you, selecting a suitable companion for your trip.

Who do you feel you know better?

Liam	Turn to 347
Panos	Turn to 297
Matt	Turn to 143
Penny	Turn to 133
None of these	Turn to 153

334

Much to your surprise, you have been rescued by the mysterious Garth Craigmillar and, as you look round the boat, you see that it is full of armed policemen. Garth doesn't seem to be in the mood for any explanations but questions you thoroughly about your activities. At the mention of the treasure, his expression, which has been quite thunderous, lightens.

'Good girl! You have saved us a lot of trouble. We'd had information that the treasure was to be lifted tonight, but had no idea where from. Now, with a bit of luck, we'll catch them red-handed!'

He snaps out a command and the boat swings in towards the little beach you have just escaped from.

Do you have some of Burke's papers?

Yes   Turn to **270**
No   Turn to **314**

335

Together you head for the nearest bar, Nikos Taverna, about half-way between the villa and the town. Sitting on the terrace on narrow wooden chairs with rush seats, sipping ice-cold *retsina* and drinking in the sunset, you begin to feel calmer. The arrival at the next table of a ferret-featured little man in a shabby grey suit captures your interest.

Slapping a small glass of *metaxa* on the table, he slumps into a chair, mopping his brow and emitting a deep, heartfelt sigh. You and Greg smile over at him politely.

'How d'ya like that?' he groans. 'Bloody marvellous. Come thousands of miles to look for a geezer who doesn't even exist . . .' From his accent you guess he is a Londoner, in fact, he looks as if he would be more at home in a greyhound stadium than on a Greek island.

'Who is it that you are looking for?' inquires Greg, trying to take a friendly interest.

'Ah . . . that'd be telling, mate,' replies the man with a confidential wink. 'Anyway, he's probably living under an assumed name, if he's got any sense.'

'Why are you looking for him?' you join in, intrigued.

The little man looks about him shiftily, then leans forward and lowers his voice, 'A *client* of mine wants to talk to him, like.' He lowers his voice still further until you can hardly make out what he is saying, 'About some money that's owed, see.' He glances behind him as if to make sure he has not been overheard.

'Are you a private detective?' you exclaim.

The man swells with self-importance. 'Could be . . . could be . . .' he replies, revelling in the attention. 'But I can't disclose the details of me work, of course, it's all very hush-hush.'

You and Greg stifle a laugh.

'Still,' he continues, knocking back his drink and getting to his feet, 'makes a change from HP defaulters and unfaithful husbands, doesn't it? Ta ra, then. Enjoy your holiday.'

Looking at the clock, you notice it is already after

6.30 and supper is at 7.30. You had better be getting back to give Penny a hand in the kitchen.

'Just think,' you say to Greg excitedly. 'I've now met a *real* private eye.'

'Huh, nothing very "private" about him!' laughs Greg. 'I'd hate him to be working for me . . . funny business. I wonder who he was sent to find.'

'We'll never know, will we?' you reply. 'We don't even know if his story was true . . .'

Turn to **299**

336

The darkness deepens the further into the tunnel you go. At one point the passage narrows so far that you can only proceed on your hands and knees. Eventually, you emerge into what feels like a small chamber, which doesn't appear to have any other exit than the way you came. You feel around for a while but find nothing. Deciding to return sometime in the future with a torch, you make your way back up the tunnel. You wander round Castro a bit more and then decide to head for home. How did you get here?

By donkey   Turn to **74**
By moped   Turn to **42**

Lose 2 Luck points for being feeble. You announce that you are going to do a spot of sunbathing whilst Panos mends the bike. Luckily, you had the foresight to put on your bikini under your shorts and T-shirt, so, selecting a secluded spot not too far from the road, you peel off your outer layers and recline amongst the bamboo. Breaking open a purple fig, plucked from a nearby tree, you suck out its syrupy red flesh. Delicious. Panos shouts across that he will have to go back to the village a few kilometres back to get some tools, and he asks you to keep an eye on the bike whilst he is gone – not that anyone can very well ride it away. You feel a stab of guilt. Perhaps you should have offered to lend a hand? Too late now.

Sometime later you are startled by an unexpected rustling in the bamboo. A suntanned face, with elegantly coiffured steel-grey hair and a white safari suit, now smeared with dirt, looms before you. The man's breath is coming in short, rasping pants, and he has a nastily cut lip as if someone has just landed him a heavy left hook.

'Listen,' he gulps, taking no notice of the fact that you are lying before him in this skimpy attire, 'there's a man following me. A thug who tried to beat me up. If you see him will you do me a favour and say you saw me head thataway across the hills towards Matelo?'

You notice that he has a distinct American accent. 'Across the hills towards Matelo,' you repeat, stunned.

The safari-suited man nods and speeds off in the opposite direction. You are definitely not going to stick around in this vulnerable position just so you can deliver a message to some marauding hood. Slipping on your clothes you start walking back towards the village. After some minutes you meet Panos on the road. He asks with annoyance why you didn't stay with the scooter.

Do you:

Tell him about your adventure?   Turn to **69**
Make some excuse and keep the
   information to yourself?   Turn to **53**

As the days pass, you settle in to your new life at the villa. The work is hard, but at least you're not on your own. Not that Penny really pulls her weight as far as the housework goes: so often she seems to have a hangover in the morning, or something wrong with her troublesome back, but she's a friendly, lively person and helps make the work pass easily. The guests are continually demanding, especially the volatile Donna Chadwick, and you sometimes find it hard to keep your temper under control. However, you remember that caring for the guests is part of your job and try to grin and bear it.

Luckily, you don't have to cater for the guests at lunchtime, so, after the morning chores are done, you are usually free until it is time to prepare the evening meal. So there is plenty of time for exploring, swimming or just lying on the beach. Much to Penny's amusement, you decide to learn how to windsurf and find an able teacher in Panos Pavlides, the extremely good-looking, sleek young Greek, who runs the windsurfing school on the main town beach. You could get to like Panos a lot, but you notice that he has an extremely possessive girlfriend who materializes out of nowhere whenever you seem to be getting close to him. Rather against your instincts, you decide to concentrate on the surfing, rather than the teacher, and use the lessons to help learn a little more Greek. You also get to know some of the students working on the dig on the little island, including the shy young Irish lad, Liam MacNamara.

You are still very intrigued by the lonely windmill on the To Limani inlet but the inhabitant, Matt Jardine, seems to be extremely elusive and, apart from meeting him fleetingly with Penny a couple of times, he remains a bit of an enigma.

Then one evening, Penny suggests going to the Black Cat disco.

Have you been to the Black Cat before?

Yes	Turn to **192**
No	Turn to **64**

339

Re-emerging from the bathroom you pause by the mirror to inspect your appearance. Snippets of an interesting-sounding conversation waft through the open porthole. You flatten yourself against the wall out of view and listen in to the discussion.

Turn to **115**

340

You're out of luck. Before you have time to guess again, the dogs decide to rid themselves of the intruders on their territory and chase you back down the path. Lose 1 Luck point.

Turn to 312

341

Lars turns out to be an appalling oarsman. After he has succeeded in dropping his oars three times and has jammed his fingers in the rowlocks, you ask permission to take over. Unwillingly he swaps places with you.

Penny has evidently decided that Lars might be worth getting to know. 'How's the dig going?' she asks with concern. Her question causes you to raise your eyebrows – this is the first time you have ever heard Penny express the slightest interest in archaeology.

'Oh, not too good,' replies Lars mournfully. 'We have discovered some very interesting old tombs, but they have all been ransacked. According to ancient records this Sanctuary housed great treasures, and a legendary gold and ivory statue of the goddess that would now be priceless.' Lars's lecture is broken up by the sound of a motorboat speeding past. At the helm is a grey-haired man in a white suit.

'Phew, that was rather too close for comfort,' you gasp as the rowing boat rocks alarmingly in the wash of the launch.

'Who was that?' asks Penny angrily. 'He nearly capsized us!'

'Orlando Burke, the director of our project,' scowls Lars. 'I'm surprised he has even bothered to come out to the dig this morning. Most of his time is spent gallivanting around with his rich friends on Koutalas's yacht.'

'He might have millionaires for friends,' answers Penny huffily, 'but he certainly doesn't have any manners.'

You have to admit she's right. On Lars's instructions you row around to the far side of the island where there is a narrow inlet. The boat secured, you begin the steep climb up to the ruined temple.

Turn to 241

342

Your luck is in. The dogs respond to your friendly advances and let you pet them. Gain 1 Luck point. You see from their collars that their names are Apollo and Icarus, which seem appropriate names for Greek guard dogs. Eventually they let you have a look round but it is clear that the occupant of the villa is not there. So, you reluctantly decide to try again another time and, bidding the dogs a friendly farewell, head off to town to do your shopping.

Turn to 55

343

From the moment Nigel disembarks from the ferry you realize that this reunion is not going to be a bed of roses. His presence disrupts the life you have begun to build for yourself on Simnos, and Matt, Panos, and even Garth, give you a wide berth whilst he is on the scene. At the end of a thoroughly miserable week Nigel begs you to return with him to England.

Are the Fates with you? Throw a die.

1–3	Turn to **173**
4–5	Turn to **149**
6	Turn to **291**

344

Once inside Castro, you can see the shape of the old town. It must have been roughly square, perched on the top of the northern cliffs. Only the outer line of fortifications show clearly now – a ragged and ruined wall several feet thick but now no more than six or seven feet at its highest point. Inside, the ground is flat and grassy, punctuated at a few points by scattered heaps of fallen masonry. Liam points out the spring, which must have been the town's main source of water, and you spend several wind-blown minutes perched on what remains of the north wall, gazing out to sea imagining the lookout searching the seas for signs of possible invaders. With the breakers crashing against the bottom of the cliff beneath you, a pleasant feeling of serenity creeps over you, only to be broken by an excited shout from Liam.

'Hey! Come over here! Look what I've found!'

When you reach him, he shows you a middle-sized boulder he has just rolled away from its former resting-place, and the gaping hole in the old wall it reveals.

'It's a secret passage! Must be. Hey, wouldn't it be great if we were the first people to have found this!' He thinks about this and then says more soberly, 'No, we can't be the first. This boulder has been moved before. It moved too easily and it's not covered with moss the way the others are. No matter. Let's have a look.'

The passage is tiny, pitch dark and musty. Who knows where it might lead – or whether you will be able to get out again. Will you go down the passage with Liam?

Yes	Turn to 298
No	Turn to 24

345

You can't find Matt anywhere and you are just about to give him up altogether when he suddenly materializes from behind a pillar.

'Where have you been?' you ask. 'I've been looking everywhere for you!'

Matt's answer is very evasive but he seems happy to take you back to the mainland. When you get there, he makes some excuse and leaves you to make your way back to the villa on your own.

Turn to 254

346

You awake suddenly in the middle of the night. The light of the full moon streams through the shutters and the only sound you hear is the gentle breeze in the trees. What time did you set your alarm for?

4.00 a.m.   Turn to 122
2.00 a.m.   Turn to 292
7.30 a.m.   Turn to 130

347

'The Goddess Aphrodite has many forms . . . Aphrodite Urania, for example, goddess of pure and ideal love . . . Aphrodite Nymphia, goddess of marriage . . .'

Liam offers a charcoaled chicken wing to the attractive French girl crouching next to him by the bonfire. She appears to be following his discourse with attention. Liam must be the only guy in the world who has thought of using ancient history and mythology as a chat-up line.

'You ought to come and visit the Sanctuary sometime . . .' he suggests casually to his pretty companion.

'Yes, I'd love to, Liam,' you butt in from behind.

'W . . . well any time you need a guide . . .' stutters Liam with surprise.

'How about tomorrow?' you suggest quickly.

Liam looks stunned by his sudden popularity with the opposite sex. Could his tactics be paying off at last? The French girl seems to have faded into the background, leaving you alone.

'OK, tomorrow,' he agrees, trying not to sound too eager. 'The boat leaves from the small cove at 9.30. Be sure to be on time. We can't wait for stragglers. It's vital to get a few good hours' digging in before the heat gets too unbearable.'

'Great. I'll be there,' you reply, delighted.

Funny, in the soft glow of the fire, Liam looks almost handsome.

Turn to 93

348

He grabs your arm and leers in an unpleasant fashion.

'Well, what have we here? A little lamb, a long way from home?' He laughs and tightens his grip on your arm. 'Give Daddy a kiss, and he'll show you the way . . .' His fat, greasy face lowers towards yours and his hot rancid breath reaches you.

How will the Fates deal with you? Throw a die.

1–3	Turn to 140
4–6	Turn to 40

349

Matt reappears looking flushed with triumph from all the celebrity attention he has been getting today. He insists on whisking you around the deck, introducing you to all the new friends he has made at the party. About four o'clock, things are beginning to wind to a close, and Matt arranges for the launch to take you both back to the shore. Liberal quantities of champagne have made him full of high spirits.

'Glad you came?' he asks, casually placing his arm around the back of the seat of the motorboat.

'Yes,' you reply, meeting his gaze evenly.

Why have you replied 'yes' to this question?

Because you find Matt Jardine
an intriguing and attractive
personality   Turn to **169**

Because you have accumulated
some interesting information
during the course of the
afternoon   Turn to **7**

350

The following day, you are amazed to discover that you are being fêted as a heroine. Virtually the whole island beats a path up to the villa to thank you for saving the treasure. The Mayor calls and offers you a substantial reward and you are showered with invitations to stay any time you want to return to Simnos. And just when you think that things couldn't possibly get any better, you receive a phone call from the Managing Director of Villalink, praising both your part in the adventure and the excellent work you have put in at the villa. In fact, they are so pleased with you that they are offering you a promotion, by making you the Area Manager for Greece! Gain 5 Luck points for the successful conclusion to your adventure.

HOW WELL DID YOU DO?

0–5 Luck points
Either you are naturally unlucky, or you have been making some bad choices. Surely you can do better than this!

6–10 Luck points
Average score. You have made some wise choices but have gone off the rails somewhere. Have another go.

11–15 Luck points
You have done very well. You must either be naturally lucky, or have been making some sensible decisions. But are you going to be satisfied with this, or will you try for an even higher score?

Over 15 Luck points
Congratulations! You have a truly adventurous character, coupled with a clear head. Luck has played a part, of course, but your ability to make the right choices has ensured your success!